Fancy 2

A Novel By

VANNA B.

HOPE
STREET
publishing

ISBN: 978-0-9853515-1-9

Photography and cover design by RJ Jacques. (www.PhotosXRJ.com)

Hope Street Publishing
P.O. Box 2705
Philadelphia, PA 19120

Acknowledgements

I'd first like to thank our good Lord for all of his continued blessings and gifts.

Thank you to the love of my life, Rodney (Akbar) for your nonstop support and for always being my rock.

And thank you to the other love of my life, my sweet Dylan. You're the greatest gift I've ever received and every day I wonder how I ever got along without you! Thank you for kissing Mommy's sore tummy and making it feel better. I know you're going to be the best big brother ever. ☺

Thank you Mom and Dad for everything. You guys make me blush how you brag and show off my work. I love it and I love you.

Thank you to all my amazing friends. I can't name you all but you certainly know who you are. Your continued support means so much to me and I'm so grateful for it.

And to all of you who read Fancy and let me know how much you enjoyed it, thank you. I love reading your e-mails and messages, hearing your thoughts and opinions. Your love and feedback has been everything to me.

To all my readers and fans, the book clubs and book groups, the seasoned authors who have offered me guidance and advice, and anyone who has helped promote and spread the word about Fancy or has allowed me to use your platform to reach new readers, thank you! Thank you for embracing me as a new author and thank you for supporting my endeavors. Stay tuned for more quality literature from Hope Street Publishing.

Sincerely,
Vanna

Chapter 1

A petite female police officer stands at the end of a glum hallway in Philadelphia's Albert Einstein hospital. She sobs quietly as she dabs her teary green eyes with a Kleen-ex. She adjusts her navy cap, attempting to regain her composure as she starts down the corridor toward the sea of dark blue uniforms congesting the maternity ward outside of room 304. A male officer turns to her with a stern look and impatiently thrusts a clipboard toward her as she approaches him.

"You okay now?" he asks demandingly.

"Yeah," she says, reaching out for the clipboard.

"Look," he says. "I know you're new to the force, but this is nothing compared to some of the things you're gonna see."

"I know, I know. It just sort of got to me because, well, she was in labor. I'm a mother too and—"

"You've got to learn to leave your emotions at home," he interrupts. "When you come to work, you have to come in with a clear head. If the captain saw you, he'd be jumping down your throat right now. He's not one for the crying and shit."

"Alright. I said I'm fine now. It won't happen again."

"Okay. Now go over there and interview the head nurse. Even though we already have the suspect in custody, we still need statements for paperwork's sake."

She looks over the first in the series of forms on the clipboard as she continues down the hall toward the nurses' station.

The victim, a 28-year-old Hispanic female was pronounced dead on the scene. Victim sustained multiple stab wounds to the abdomen while in labor, she reads. *The unborn child was also killed.* The officer shakes her head. "Sick," she whispers to herself, "Just sick."

Chapter 2

"So...Alan Schwartz. You're the hit man we've been trying to find for the past four months!" a disheveled looking detective exclaims, entering the interrogation room and slamming the door closed behind him.

"You might as well save your breath," says the thin, bald man sitting handcuffed at the table. "I won't say anything else until my lawyer gets here."

"Oh, I don't think there's much he'll be able to do for you."

"You must not know who he is, then."

"Garett Smith, best criminal lawyer in the city of Philadelphia. We're very familiar with the slimy bastard. He's helped a lot of guilty scumbags go free. Unfortunately for you, though, you won't be one of them."

Schwartz chuckles and shakes his head, leaning back in his chair.

"Go ahead and laugh. You won't be doing much of that when the boys in the bing get wind of what you're in for. Did you really think you would get away with murdering a helpless pregnant woman and an innocent fetus?"

"I don't know what you're talking about."

"Yeah, you have no idea. But you just so happened to have her blood on your shirt."

"I told you a man wearing a doctor's lab coat bumped into me in the hallway."

"Oh, I see. And you were in the hospital's maternity ward because...?"

"I like babies," Schwartz says sarcastically. "I just wanted to take a peek at the newborns in the nursery. Is that a crime?"

"You think you're real slick. We found the murder weapon and the lab coat you stashed in the janitor's closet. And you did a pretty good job of keeping them free of your prints and DNA this time. The thing is your fingerprints are a match to murder weapons in three other open cases."

"You don't have anything on me."

"The name Grant Fuller ring a bell?"

"Not at all."

"His brother, Hank Fuller?"

"Never heard of him."

"How about Vincent Stouffer."

"Nope, sorry."

"You were paid to murder all these men. We've even got witnesses for two of them. You're going to jail for the rest of your rotten, miserable life."

Schwartz shifts nervously in his seat.

"Unless..." says the detective, "Well, maybe we can work something out if—"

"If what?"

"If you tell us who hired you to kill these men and the girl. Then, and only then, will we be able to reduce your sentence. Help us help you. We know these murders were business...not personal. Someone – I'm guessing several different someones

– paid you indecent amounts of moo-la to take these people out. And we want all their names."

Several minutes later the detective emerges from the interrogation room.

"He give up any names?" asks another detective waiting outside the door.

"You bet your ass he did. Sang like a bird. And you'll never guess who ordered the Spanish girl hit."

Chapter 3

Maribel sits on the sofa with her mother, Anna, cradling her four-day-old newborn son in her arms. She gazes at him lovingly as he quietly sleeps.

"Yep, that's my little papito," Anna says, stroking the baby's fine black hair. "He looks just like his abuela."

"I think he looks like me," Maribel says.

"And where do you think you get your good looks from? Everyone always says you look like your mama."

"I guess so. He really doesn't look like Aaron, though. He's so light. I wonder if he'll get darker as he gets older."

"I don't know. He barely looks Moreno at all. Our Boricua genes are strong."

Anna picks up the remote control and changes the TV station to channel 10 for the three o'clock news, which is just beginning with breaking news.

Maribel's attention is snatched from the baby by the news story:

Police have arrested Philadelphia 76ers point guard Aaron Jameson for conspiracy to murder. A man says he was paid $100,000 by Jameson to murder a woman Monday while she was in labor at Albert Einstein Hospital. The woman, 28-year-old Araceli Ramirez, was to give birth to *her second child, but both mother and child were killed in the brutal stabbing. Ramirez leaves behind a husband and 5-year-old daughter.*

Maribel can hardly believe what she is hearing and seeing as she stares at the photo of the beautiful slain woman on the television screen that bears a striking resemblance to her own image.

"Oh my God!" she gasps, covering her mouth with her hand in shock. She turns to Anna, who is staring back at her silently, eyes and mouth wide. "I'm gonna be sick," Maribel says, quickly handing the swaddled newborn to her mother and dashing for the front door. Anna sets the infant in his bassinet before going to check on her daughter. She finds Maribel doubled over on the cement steps in tears.

"Mari, you okay?"

"No, I'm not! Aaron sent that guy to kill *me*!"

"You don't know that. How do you know it's even true? That guy could have framed Aaron. Why would he want to kill you?"

"Come on, Mom. You know he wanted no part of the baby! He made that very clear when I told him I was pregnant. I never thought he'd go that far, though. I mean, I knew he was messed in the head but I never thought he was capable of something so sick and evil." Maribel shakes her head as she sits down on the top step. "That poor girl and her baby!" she cries out. "Innocent lives taken for no reason at all. While I was giving birth they were down the hall being murdered! Now I know why all those cops were there. And that whole thing with Brittany…she was trying to help Aaron do his dirty work…that bitch!"

"What are you talking about?"

Maribel thinks back to four days ago. "I hadn't seen her in months when she just showed up at my job out of the blue. My water broke right then while she was standing there so I asked her to take me to the hospital. But she wasn't driving toward Einstein. I told her she was going the wrong way and she ignored me and just kept heading in the same direction, so I knew something was wrong. I grabbed the wheel and when we hit the guardrail I got out and flagged down a ride to the hospital."

"Jesus, Mari. Why didn't you tell me?"

"I didn't know what it was about at the time, but it all makes sense now."

"God was watching over you," says a tearful Anna, wrapping her arms around her daughter. "I'm just grateful you made it through this. I don't know what I would do if something happened to you or the baby. I'm glad you're both safe."

"I am too," Maribel whispers, hugging her mother back tightly. They walk inside the house and peer into the bassinet where the sleeping infant is lying. Normally she would not risk interrupting his slumber by picking him up, but right now she *needs* to feel him in her arms.

Chapter 4

The way Maribel felt four days ago when she laid her eyes on her son for the first time, was the happiest she had ever been. Never before had she experienced such intense love and pure joy, and she knew that while even "love" and "joy" inadequately described what she felt for him, they would have to suffice simply because no other, more accurate words existed.

She had taken him into her arms and instantly fell in love, crying tears of joy. She gazed at his angelic face and decided she would name him Shawn in honor of her beloved fallen friend. But Maribel's tears of joy turned into tears of despair as she thought about Shawna and wished she were there to meet the tender angel named after her.

One of her nurses, a tall and muscled fellow with a dazzling bright smile and skin the color of a Special Dark Hershey's bar, noticed Maribel seemed troubled.

"It's normal to feel a little sad," he said, as he checked her blood pressure. "A lot of women experience postpartum depression."

"No. It's not that. I'm just thinking of someone I wish was here to see the baby. A friend of mine that passed away."

"Oh, I see. Yes, that is tough. I'm sorry your friend can not be here, but you know what? I bet they are smiling down on you two from Heaven."

"I bet you're right," Maribel smiled, imagining Shawn as an angel watching over them. "Thank you."

"I'd just hate for you to be sad during such an occasion. You should be celebrating. Is your husband on his way?" Maribel's blank stare let him know she had no husband to speak of. "Or your boyfriend? The baby's father?"

"No, he won't be coming. It's a complicated situation. As a matter of fact there have been a lot of confusing and strange things going on lately."

"I'm a very good listener if you care to talk about it."

Maribel watched as he took a seat in the chair next to her bed. *He is gorgeous*, she had thought to herself. *He should be in magazines and on billboards modeling Calvin Klein underwear.*

"My name is Dolo, by the way." His face was kind as he gazed at her, patiently waiting for her to speak, and she could see that he was sincere about his willingness to listen.

"Well Dolo, this is going to sound crazy, but okay."

Maribel took a deep breath before beginning to recount the bizarre story of how she went into labor while working her supermarket cashier job and how she managed to make it to the hospital despite the fact that her old "friend" Brittany tried to sabotage everything by attempting to drive her elsewhere. Although Dolo was a stranger, Maribel found it so easy and natural to talk to him, and before she knew it, she had opened up about her failed relationship with Aaron, her guilt over Shawn's passing, and her near-death encounter with Bella and the Latin Queens.

Dolo listened intently and then there was a long silence as he internalized all she had said.

"Wow, you've been through a lot," he finally said. "I guess we have that in common. We're both very lucky to be here." Maribel's curious look, prompted him to follow suit and open up about his past.

"I was 12 years old when the soldiers took me and my brother and sister from our small village near Monrovia."

"Liberia?" she asked, remembering her African geography.

"Yes. We were at the marketplace. My sister was 14; my brother was only nine. The soldiers took us along with many other children, some as young as six. They put guns in our hands and trained us to be killers in the war."

"The Liberian civil war," she realized out loud. She had once seen a documentary about the war and the child soldiers forced to fight in it. She never imagined she would be face to face with one of the survivors.

"I've seen things no child should have to witness; children beaten to death and slaughtered with machetes. Young girls raped and maimed. My own brother and sister gunned down before my eyes. Even worse were the things I had to do to stay alive. I've been forced to take many innocent lives. Shed enough blood to fill Lake Piso."

Maribel immediately felt silly and somewhat embarrassed for thinking she'd had it so bad, when it was obvious the adversity she had known paled in comparison to what Dolo had been through.

"I don't know how I survived," he continued. "At times I didn't even want to. But thoughts of my mom and my little sister Suah kept me going. They are all I have left now."

Maribel watched Dolo's eyes as he recounted his tragic past. They were cold and still and she could see the sheer pain within them. It was difficult to imagine him being a killer, skilled in the art of death dealing, when he seemed nothing less than pure-hearted and good. He was a walking paradox. So kind and gentle by nature, yet unable to wash the blood from his hands or remove from his psyche the horrid memories of the countless heinous acts he had committed. He was so genuine and open, yet so mysterious. She was instantly drawn to Dolo and yearned to know more about him and what made him tick.

"Are your mom and sister still in Africa?"

"Yes. I've tried to convince my mom to move here but she is totally against it. She says she will never leave her homeland."

"How'd you end up in the U.S.?"

"I was one of the lucky ones relocated here by an aide group. They put us in foster homes and set us up with jobs. I cleaned buildings and worked at a car wash for years so I could put myself through school. And here I am."

"That's awesome, Dolo. I was in in school for nursing at one point. I wish I would have never left. I would love to go back one day."

"You should. If it's a dream of yours, don't give up on it for anything."

She smiled at his encouraging advice. "You're right, Dolo. I will definitely have to pick up where I left off once I get back on my feet. What about you? What is your dream? Is this it?"

"I enjoy nursing. I love helping people. But this job is also a stepping-stone to help me achieve my ultimate goal. I've been saving up so I can open a job training and placement center back home. Many of the former child soldiers weren't as lucky as I was. They never got the chance to get an education and still are living in poverty, unable to find work and struggling to support their families. One day I'll help change that."

Like Maribel, Dolo had known loss. He had witnessed and experienced cruelty and inhumanity at its worst. But he didn't allow his awful past to jade him. Somehow he still managed to remain gentle and compassionate after such an ordeal. Throughout her stay at the hospital, he had provided Maribel with unexpected, yet greatly appreciated comfort and companionship. Before leaving the hospital at the end of his shift, he gave Maribel his phone number and told her she could call him if she ever needed to talk. She gladly accepted his digits and promised to use them soon, but in all the chaos of having a newborn she had not been able to find the time to do so. Until now.

Chapter 5

After seeing the mind-blowing news story about Aaron, Maribel needs someone to talk to more than ever. She looks down at the piece of paper she is holding in her left hand and picks up her cell phone with her right. *Two-six-seven*, she begins, dialing the numbers inscribed on the paper.

"Hello?" Dolo answers in his distinct Liberian accent after the second ring.

"Hi, Dolo. This is—"

"Hi, Maribel," he interrupts. "How are you?"

"I'm fine," she answers, slightly surprised. "And you?"

"I'm doing well. How's little Shawn?"

"Oh, he's great. Eating and sleeping up a storm."

"That's good to hear," Dolo chuckles. "I'm glad you called me."

"Yeah, I was just thinking of getting out of the house today. Wanted to take the baby out for some fresh air and figured maybe you might like to join us."

"Sure, I'd love to."

They arrange to meet for a stroll in the park and lunch. After hanging up with Dolo, Maribel slips on a pastel pink and white striped tank top with a blue denim skirt and white leather flat sandals. She is excited about seeing Dolo, but doesn't want to give off the impression of trying too hard, as she isn't looking to take their relationship anywhere beyond the friend zone. She opts for a ponytail, leaving a few curly tendrils loose to frame her face, which she leaves natural except for a little lip gloss and mascara. She dresses Shawn in a green romper with embroidered frogs and a matching hat.

As she nears the center of Rittenhouse Square Park, she spots Dolo sitting on a bench. He stands when he sees her and flashes his big, sparkling smile as she approaches him. She can't help but feel the familiar nervous flutter of butterflies in her stomach as she notices how incredibly handsome he looks in his blue jeans and crisp tee, the bright white matching his pearly teeth and contrasting beautifully against his smooth, chocolate skin. *Calm down*, she reminds herself. *He's just a friend and that's the way it's going to stay.*

"Hello, Maribel. Beautiful day, huh?"

"Yeah, the weather is perfect."

"And hello to you, Shawn," he says, stooping down in front of the stroller. "How are you today, little man?"

Shawn stares silently at Dolo with his big brown eyes. They stroll around the park chatting for about a half an hour during which Maribel fills Dolo in with the details of the news story she had seen the previous day. After working up their appetites, they decide to check out a nearby restaurant and grab a bite to eat. As they walk up

Walnut Street, Maribel notices a black, tinted Rolls Royce Phantom has slowed down to cruise along at the same pace that they are walking. She turns to Dolo to see if he has also noticed the car but he continues walking and talking, seemingly oblivious to the creeping vehicle. When she turns to the street again the car is still there, coasting along with them. She quickly pulls the stroller to a halt and the car also stops suddenly.

"Is everything okay?" Dolo asks, finally noticing the black car. Frozen, Maribel fearfully stares at the car in silence, half expecting the door to open and appease her curiosity and fear. Just then the driver of the van behind the Phantom lays on his horn, startling Maribel and causing her to jump as her heart thumps against the walls of her chest. The van driver throws his hands up, signaling his irritation at the car's sudden stop. The Phantom speeds off up the street and disappears around the corner.

As she and Dolo watch its trailing taillights in bewilderment, Maribel breaks out in a sweat and begins to feel panicky. She doesn't like how vulnerable and exposed she feels standing there out in the open, and all she wants to do is get Shawn home to safety as soon as possible.

"I gotta go," she nervously says to Dolo before running off down the street, leaving him standing in the middle of Walnut Street alone. "I'll call you later!" she yells, without looking back. A confused Dolo watches as his lunch date abandons him, and he can't help but wonder, *what the hell just happened?*

Chapter 6

Three days pass and Maribel still does not know what to make of the incident with the black Phantom. She considers the possibility that Aaron may still be out to get her and the baby, but from inside of his jail cell? *I guess anything is possible,* she thinks to herself. The only other person that comes to mind is Bella, who is also incarcerated. *Could she have sent one of her gang members?* After a while she begins to wonder if perhaps she is simply overthinking things. Maybe she had overreacted out of fear and paranoia due to the things that had happened to her before. She reasons that it was probably just nothing. Maybe someone thought she or Dolo looked familiar. Hell, it could have even been a jealous ex of his for all she knows. She remembers that she had not fulfilled her promise to call Dolo and is reaching for her phone to do so when she is interrupted by the sound of her mother yelling up the stairs.

"Mari! Ven aquí."

As she descends the staircase she sees Anna holding a beautiful bouquet of yellow roses.

"Ooooh they're pretty, Mom. You got a new boyfriend you're not telling me about?"

"I was hoping they were from a new secret admirer but nope, actually they're for you."

"For me?"

She reads the card attached to the bouquet: *For my Fancy girl. See you soon.*

The only person she imagines could have sent them is Dolo. She doesn't recall telling him her former alias, but she figures she must have unknowingly mentioned it while they spoke in the hospital. She was a little loopy from the meds anyway, she supposes, so she probably just doesn't remember that bit of the conversation.

She dials him up, lifting the bouquet to her nose and taking in the sweet scent of the roses.

"Hi, Maribel."

"Hey, Dolo. I just wanted to thank you for the roses. They're beautiful."

There is a moment of silence before he responds. "I wish I could take the credit for it, but I didn't send any roses."

"You didn't?"

"No, I guess I'm not the only one eyeing you. Not surprisingly though. You're a lovely lady…"

Dolo continues talking but Maribel is no longer hearing what he is saying. She is still stuck on the fact that the flowers are not from him. *Who else could have possibly sent them?* She has not dealt with anyone since Aaron and besides, to her knowledge, no one knows where she lives. She averts her attention back to the phone conversation just in time to hear Dolo invite her to dinner that evening. She says yes and they arrange for him to pick her up at her mother's at seven.

Chapter 7

Dolo arrives at seven on the dot with an enormous bouquet of purple and white orchids. Maribel can't help but smile, realizing his objective was to outdo whoever sent the roses – a goal certainly achieved.

"Nice," she laughs, taking the huge bouquet. "Thank you."

"Hey, I see I've got to step my game up," Dolo says, "I've got some competition."

Maribel ignores his comment and after briefly introducing Dolo to her mother, she gives Anna the orchids to put in water and kisses Shawn goodbye. Then her and Dolo set off into the warm summer night.

He opens the passenger door to his gray Dodge Charger and allows Maribel to get in before letting himself in. When he slides into his seat, she finally gets a good look at his attire for the evening: tan khakis and an off-white military-style button up shirt – the kind with different embroidered patches. The shirt's short sleeves are cuffed and hug his muscular biceps. Maribel has to admit to herself, *the man is damn sexy.* She is glad she opted for something a little more showy this time: a long, flowing white dress that contrasts perfectly against her sun-bronzed skin, accessorized with all gold jewelry. Paired with strappy gold heels that help

21

accentuate her legs, she knows she is foxy and thinks that her and Dolo look great together.

He takes her to a favorite spot of his, Charleston's Kitchen, an upscale soul food restaurant in Manayunk, with a romantic ambiance and delicious food. There is a live jazz band playing tunes of classic musicians like Louie Armstrong and Ella Fitzgerald. They relax and enjoy the music over their appetizers and a bottle of wine.

"The way you ran off on me the other day, I was kind of surprised when you called me."

"I told you I would. And sorry for running off. It had nothing to do with you."

"Well, I'm glad to hear it. What have you been up to?"

"Not much. Just taking care of Shawn. He amazes me more and more each day. Today I stuck my tongue out at him and he stuck his out back at me! I was lucky enough to get a pic." Maribel shows Dolo the photo in her phone and he laughs.

"Your little man really is something."

"So what you been getting into these past few days?"

"Work, mostly. And got to finish up a couple of models I've been working on."

"Models?"

"Airplanes. I like to put together model airplanes in my spare time."

"Oh, cool. Sounds like fun. What made you take up that hobby?"

"I've always liked airplanes. When I was a boy there was an airbase not too far from my village. The planes would fly over us really low, and I'd get all excited and jump up and down every time I saw one. I had this little blue toy plane I'd always play with. Man, I played with that thing so much something was always falling off of it…the propeller, the rudder, the wings. I glued it back together so many times. Had to paint it every time the paint started chipping off. I think that's why I love putting together the models so much."

When their food arrives, Dolo leaves his seat across from her and slides into the booth with her.

"I want to be close to you," he says. "I feel like I'm so far away over there." Maribel does not protest. The air conditioner in the restaurant is on blast and the heat from his body is just what she needs to warm her up. On top of that, his cologne smells amazing – a fresh, clean fragrance in which she can detect a hint of sandalwood. When they eat their entrees, Dolo feeds her forkfuls from his plate and dabs the corner of her mouth with his napkin. She loves all the attention he is giving her and when he asks her to dance, she gladly accepts. They join the other couples on the dance floor swaying in sync with the bellowing saxophone and sweet piano.

The evening is going so perfectly Maribel doesn't want it to end. Eventually it is time for them to leave the restaurant and she finds herself low-spirited, wishing their date could last just a little longer. She is happy when, during the ride home, Dolo suggests they continue their night by stopping somewhere for drinks. They choose a random neighborhood lounge not too far from her mother's house. The bar area is crowded, but they are soon able to slide in and place their drink order. Maribel requests a Corona while Dolo orders Remy on the rocks. The two are content, drinking, conversing and enjoying each other's company. Everything is going smoothly until a drunken man grabs Maribel's butt. When Dolo sees this he instantly loses it.

"Fuck wrong with you, boy?!" he yells, jumping in the man's face, drill sergeant style, his deep, booming voice causing everyone close enough to hear it over the blaring music to turn their attention toward the altercation in progress.

"Damn homie, chillll," the drunken man slurs, backing up and attempting to diffuse the situation. "I ain't know that was ya bitch."

The fire in Dolo's eyes makes it obvious to the man that he has made a poor choice in words. But before he even knows what has hit him, he is laid down flat by Dolo's right hook. His two friends, who had been trying to order drinks down at the other end of the bar, come rushing over angrily when they realize their friend has just been knocked out cold.

Maribel's brain finally begins to fight through the alcoholic daze to catch up and process what is happening. When she sees the man's two friends approaching, she is afraid that they will gang up on Dolo and beat him down. She clutches the neck of her nearly empty Corona bottle tightly, preparing to use it as a weapon, if necessary.

When the rest of the bar catches wind of the fight, everyone rushes over to crowd around and watch. In the midst of all the chaos Maribel is pushed and shoved and finds herself behind a bunch of rowdy, hollering spectators. She makes her way back through the crowd just in time to see the third man falling unconscious to the ground. Dolo is standing over him, chest heaving and fists clenched, waiting for the man to pop back up. But he doesn't. Nor do the other two. His eyes dart around the room looking for Maribel, and when he sees her he grabs her by the hand and they exit the building, all eyes on them.

Maribel is shocked by Dolo's reaction. Despite what he had told her about his past in Liberia, she never imagined she would witness him behave so violently. He's always so calm and sweet; so kind and considerate. He had demonstrated nothing but perfect acts of chivalry all night, and had practically treated her like royalty, never failing to pull out her chair or open every door for her. But when he saw her being disrespected the gentleman quickly disappeared and the beast came out. He had rushed to her aide as her personal knight in shining armor. She loves the gentleman in him but, to her surprise, she also finds herself slightly turned on by Dolo's rough side. She appreciates that it was all for the sake of protecting her and upholding her honor. As if he is reading her mind, Dolo breaks the silence and says, "I'm sorry you had to see me like that, Love, but there was no way I was going to let that man disrespect you like that. Not on my watch."

Love? The new nickname he has bestowed upon her makes her a little uneasy. In fact, her own growing feelings toward him, make her downright nervous, especially knowing she has vowed to herself not to fall in love and to make sure Dolo remains just a friend. *But, it's not like he said he loves me*, she reasons, brushing aside her concerns, while making a mental note to get her emotions in check.

When Dolo drops Maribel off at 1:40 AM he walks her up to the door to see her in safely. They stare at each other as Dolo moves closer to her to kiss her goodbye. Maribel is preparing to feel his lips touch hers, but then she remembers that he is to remain a friend, and nothing more. At the last second she turns her head abruptly, forcing him to kiss her cheek instead. Though Dolo is initially a bit confused, he figures maybe he is just moving too fast for her. They say goodnight and share a hug instead.

Dolo releases her from the embrace and cringes as he removes his hand from the small of her back. He tries to hide his anguish but it is obvious to Maribel that he is in pain.

"You okay?" she asks, concerned.

"Yeah, I'm fine," he lies, examining his swollen, bruised right hand.

"Dolo, look at your hand! You must have hurt it in that bar fight. You better go to the hospital. It might be broken."

"Nah, it probably just needs a little ice."

"It looks bad. Promise me you'll at least get it checked out?"

Dolo sighs and reluctantly nods in agreement. He can't help but smile as he walks to his car, realizing he's been forced into a promise, but glad to know that Maribel cares enough to do so.

Once inside the house, Maribel can hear Shawn crying and the sound of Anna's feet pacing back and forth across the floor. She walks up the stairs to see her frazzled-looking mother bouncing Shawn in her arms and patting his back, trying unsuccessfully to calm him down.

"Finally!" Anna exclaims, thrusting Shawn into her arms. "I hope you had fun staying out all night getting drunk with your new boyfriend."

Maribel rolls her eyes and huffs. "Mom, please. You act like I go out every night. This is the first time I've been out since I had the baby."

"And let's make it the last until you find another sitter."

"I thought he'd be asleep."

"Well he's not. He's been fed, changed, and has still been screaming for over an hour."

Maribel holds Shawn close to her, and begins rocking him gently. He stops crying right away.

"I guess we know what he wanted now...his mother. Next time just tell your little boyfriend to take you out in the daytime so you can bring your son with you."

"We just went out with Shawn the other day. And he's not my boyfriend."

"Obviously he's trying to be. And I don't see why you don't just let him. He seems like a nice enough guy. And besides..." *Here it comes,* Maribel thinks, knowing her mother can seldom say anything nice without following it with a "but" or a "besides."

"And besides, since you're not working anymore, you could certainly use some financial help."

"Oh boy, here we go!"

"I'm serious, Mari! He's got a good nursing job at the hospital. LPNs make decent money. And I'm sure he'd be more than happy to toss you a few coins every now and then. Tell him instead of spending all that money on flowers he can just give it to you for the baby."

"I'm not trying to get into a relationship right now, Mom. After everything that's happened with Aaron I'm not about to be so quick to trust another man."

"He's not Aaron, Mari. Don't make him pay for your ex's mistakes. He seems very sweet."

"Yes, he does. But Aaron was just as sweet in the beginning and look what kind of person he turned out to be. When you first meet somebody they don't show you the real them. They show you what they want you to see."

"Yeah, I know you know alllll about that, Miss *Fancy*!"

Maribel has to laugh at her mother's sarcastic comment. "Haha! You throwing shots, Mom?"

"I'm just saying! It's okay, though. You don't have to give Dolo a chance if you don't want to. But you've got to do something, Mari. You know damn well I don't make enough at my little admin gig to support all three of us. Why don't you go down to the welfare office tomorrow? Get you some food stamps and some cash so at least you can help out a little. They might even help you pay for daycare so you can go back to the working at Val-U Rite."

Maribel knows her mother is right. With Anna working a 9 to 5 again there is no one to watch Shawn during the day, so she has not been able to return to her cashier job at the market. She is grateful that Anna has been supporting the two of them and allowing them to stay with her, and she knows it is only right that she start bringing in some type of money.

"Okay, Mom, I'll go down there tomorrow."

Chapter 8

The next day Maribel is hung-over but she keeps the promise she made to her mother to go apply for public assistance. She sets Shawn in his stroller and starts the six-block trek to the welfare office. It's a 98-degree July day and the sun is beating down on her, making her sweat. While walking, she becomes a little nervous when she sees a black Rolls Royce approaching from up the street. It appears to be the same model as the one she had seen while she was downtown with Dolo, but it doesn't stop or slow down. It continues right past her and she shakes off her nervousness, again dismissing it as paranoia.

When she is just around the corner from the office, she takes a pair of dark sunglasses and an Olney High baseball cap from her bag and puts them on before hurrying around the corner and into the building. She expects to walk into an air-conditioned facility and get some relief from the sweltering heat, but once inside, she is sure the place is just as hot as outside, if not hotter. There is obviously no air conditioning, just a bunch of open windows attempting to let in whatever rare breeze blows through, a few fans circulating the stale, musty air, and a bunch of sweaty, miserable and complaining people. The place is packed and the line to the front counter is wrapped around the room. Maribel stands in the back of it, preparing for the long, uncomfortable wait ahead of her. She plays with Shawn to attempt to keep him happy and occupied, but the heat soon starts to make him cranky and he joins several other babies who are already crying. Together they form a sad chorus, singing a tearful melody of woe, but no one seems as irritated by their screams as they are with the rising temperature in the room. Maribel removes Shawn's shirt and fans him with her cap to try to cool him down.

"Fancy?" she hears a female voice say from behind her. *Shit*, she thinks, groaning quietly. She had been hoping not to run into anyone she knows. "Is that you, Fancy?"

She turns around and is face to face with the last person she expects to see in her neighborhood.

"Trinity?"

"It *is* you!" Trinity squeals. "How are you, girl? Oh my God, you had the baby! Awww, look at him. He's adorable!"

"What are you doing around here, Trinity? I thought you were staying with Rick in South Philly?"

"Yeah, I am. But I can't get welfare over there because him and his mom are already using his address to get it."

"Oh."

"So I'm using someone else's address," she whispers, looking around suspiciously. "My homie on Rising Sun. But anyway, how you been?"

"I'm fine," Maribel responds dryly.

31

"Damn, Fancy, don't sound so happy to see me," Trinity says sarcastically.

"Well, Trinity, if you recall you *did* almost have me killed – while I was pregnant!"

"You act like I maliciously sent Bella after you. I really didn't have a choice, though! She was gonna kill *my* ass if I didn't tell her where you were. But I wasn't gonna let you get hurt. Why you think I showed up wit Rick's burner?"

Maribel huffs, glancing impatiently over Trinity's head.

"Look, I know it was fucked up," continues Trinity, "but in the end didn't I come through for you? If that had never happened Bella would still be out here making your life a living Hell instead of locked up in a cell where her psycho ass belongs. You were a good friend to me, Fancy. Gave me a roof over my head when I really needed one, and I appreciate you looking out for me with my drug problem and stepping up to Bella like you did. That was some courageous shit to do...crazy, but brave."

Trinity laughs and Maribel can't help cracking a smile, too.

"You know she's about to get out, though, right?" Trinity asks, no longer laughing.

"Bella?" Maribel inquires, her expression quickly turning from an amused one to a worried one. "But how? She had warrants. I thought she was supposed to be away for a while."

"She was. But apparently she cut some kind of deal by snitching on the heads of the whole damn

Latin Kings & Queens organization. Gave up the national headquarters in Chicago and they're letting the bitch go."

"What? How you know that?"

"My cousin's baby mom was locked up wit her."

"When's she supposed to be getting out?"

"Soon. She might even be out already, but I doubt you'll have to worry about her. From what I hear there's a pretty hefty bounty on her head and I'm sure she'll be tucked away in the boondocks somewhere under witness protection and all that."

Maybe. Huge droplets of sweat roll from Maribel's forehead as she pictures the black car that has been lurking around. *Could it have been Bella? It had to have been! Who else could it be?*

"You okay?" Trinity asks. "You look shook."

"I'm wondering if I will run into her again."

"I'm tellin' ya, girl…I seriously doubt it. She'll probably have a whole new identity and shit. If she wants to live, she'll def be laying as low as she possibly can, 'cause if the gang gets a hold of her, it's curtains."

And if Bella gets a hold of me, it's curtains.

"But hey, don't lose no sleep over it, okay? That's just what I heard. It might not even be true. You know people like to talk shit."

"I guess."

"Anyway though, you gonna give me your number so we can keep in touch?"

33

"I don't know, Trin."

"Come on, you see I'm trying to get my shit together. I stopped working at Star's – that's why I'm in here – and I haven't been taking no E-pills or coke or anything. I left all that shit alone. I need some positive people in my corner, girl. Can we be cool again?"

Maribel takes a deep breath before beginning. "I guess so. But look, if you start getting back into any of your old ways, we're cutting ties again – for good! I got a son now and I don't have time for no nonsense or BS."

"I told you, Fancy, I'm good!"

"And don't call me Fancy! I don't go by that name anymore. I use my real name…"

"Maribel," they say at the same time.

"I remember," Trinity smiles.

"But what should I call you? " Maribel asks, realizing she's never known Trinity's government name. "What's your real na—"

"Uh-uh," she cuts her off. "Just call me Trinity. My real name is Cambodian and nobody can ever pronounce the shit right."

"Ba-fa-chan Key-oh!" Trinity's caseworker yells from the front counter, botching her name terribly.

"You see what I mean?" Trinity says to Maribel with a twisted mouth and raised eyebrow.

"It's Bop-a-chan, damn it!" she yells across the crowded room, her loud, high-pitched voice causing everyone to turn and look. "I told yall mothafuckas the damn PH don't make no F sound! Shit!"

The two giggle while exchanging numbers and agree to do more catching up later on.

Chapter 9

Maribel returns home from the welfare office and is greeted by the sweet and spicy, mouth-watering aroma of sofrito. Anna has dinner on the stove and is putting away groceries.

"You went food shopping, Mom?" Maribel asks, looking at the table full of grocery bags.

"No," Anna replies.

"I did," she hears a familiar voice say.

Maribel looks around for the source and Dolo, who is sitting on the other side of the table, sticks his head out from behind a brown paper shopping bag.

"Thanks, Dolo, but that wasn't necessary."

"I just wanted to help out. I know you aren't working at the moment, and I figured everyone needs groceries."

Maribel looks over the food Dolo has bought: milk, eggs, bread and all the essentials as well as meats, fruits, vegetables, snacks and even baby food and cereal for Shawn, who is not yet old enough to eat solid food. She smiles at the kind gesture; she appreciates him thinking of her and her family and helping them out.

"I think it was very thoughtful of you Dolo," her mother says.

"It was," agrees Maribel. "Thank you."

"You're quite welcome."

Dolo takes out a teddy bear he got for Shawn and is playing with him when Anna pulls Maribel into the dining room and hands her a thick envelope with "Fancy" written on it.

"Somebody dropped this in the mail slot." Her mother watches while she opens it and both of their eyes grow large when they see what is inside – a bunch of hundred dollar bills. Maribel counts them are there are 25 of them totaling $2,500.

"Who do you think sent it, Mari?"

"I have absolutely no idea! Must be the same person that sent the roses."

"Maybe it's Aaron."

"Impossible. He's in jail, remember?"

"Yeah, but he could have had someone else do it."

"Are you forgetting that the man tried to have me killed?!"

"I know. I'm just thinking maybe he feels bad about it now. You know prison makes people change. People find God, Allah, Buddha…they realize their sins, and do total 360s when they're in there. He's had some time to think and maybe he's sorry and is sending the money to help care for the baby."

"I don't know. I guess it's possible. That's the only explanation that would make sense, but I still don't believe it."

"Well anyway, that was really nice of Dolo to bring the groceries. He's a good one, Mari. You ought to give him a chance."

They walk back into the kitchen where Dolo is saying goodbye to Shawn and preparing to leave.

"Aren't you going to stay for dinner, Dolo?" Anna asks, turning off the burner and removing the pot from the stove.

"Yeah, stay and eat. My mom's cooking is the best."

"Sure, I'd love to. Thanks."

"Well I have a nail appointment," Anna says, grabbing her bag and rushing out of the kitchen before adding, "Help yourselves, guys. Just save a little for me."

Maribel makes a plate for each of them and a bottle for Shawn. When Dolo reaches out to take his plate she notices the cast on his hand.

"Awww, Dolo – your hand."

"Yeah, you were right; it's fractured. I'm glad you talked me into going to the hospital."

"How long do they think it'll take to heal?"

"Four to six weeks, most likely. I'll be glad, too; already anxious to get back to my airplanes."

"Oh riiiight, I guess it's hard to put all those tiny parts together, with only your left hand."

"Yep, pretty much impossible."

"Well, I've never built any model airplanes before – come to think of it, I've never built any model anything before – but I could come over and try to help you put some together if you want."

"Sounds like a plan," Dolo smiles.
They enjoy their food quietly for several minutes until finally Dolo breaks the silence.

"I'm going home." The statement is unexpected and bewildering, and Maribel is like a deer caught in headlights, frozen with wide eyes and a mouth full of food.

"Right now?" she asks, the words muffled by rice and beans. "You haven't even finished eating."

"No," he laughs. "I'm going home to Liberia…in a few months."

"For good?"

"No, just for a visit. I'm gonna stay for two weeks."

"Aw, that's nice Dolo. You excited? I know you'll be glad to see your mom and sister."

"Yeah, I'm really looking forward to seeing them. It's been years. You're so lucky you have your family right here with you and get to see them every day."

"I never really thought about it before but I guess you're right."

"When I go to visit the hardest part is always when I have to leave to come back. I know I'm gonna miss them so much. Even the village. I miss the simplicity of life back home. Even though some don't have running water and are very poor by American standards, the people are just so much more…happy."

Maribel loves listening to Dolo talk. She appreciates his sentimental side and how he values the simpler things in life like family and true happiness. *Not too many like him*, she thinks. When it is time for him to leave, she sets Shawn in his playpen and escorts Dolo to the door.

"Thanks again for the groceries," she says. "I'm glad you stayed."

"It's no problem at all and please tell your mom I said thank you for the delicious meal. Bye, Maribel."

As Dolo is walking out, Maribel grabs his hand to stop him. He turns to face her and, standing on the tips of her toes, she reaches up to kiss his full, soft lips. Her heart flutters and she looks down at floor sheepishly to hide her blushing cheeks. Despite her attempts to brush aside her feelings for him, something about Dolo makes her feel like a schoolgirl with a high school crush; a feeling she hasn't felt since Aaron; a feeling that she reminds herself led to a relationship that ended in disaster. And while she enjoys the kiss she finds herself instantly regretting it.

Chapter 10

The following day Dolo calls offering to take Maribel up on her offer to help him with his model airplane crafts. She agrees and he picks her up to bring her over to his house in Germantown. When she enters his home her eyes are immediately drawn upwards to the dozens of model planes hanging above her head. And as they walk from the living room to the dining room, she is amazed to see the whole ceiling of the first floor is adorned with the dangling miniature aircrafts.

"Wow, how long have you been putting these together? You've done so many."

"I started doing them when I was in nursing school, whenever I had spare time between class and work, and it's remained a hobby of mine ever since."

"So what kind of plane are we doing today?"

Dolo pulls out a chair for her at the dining room table and extends his hand toward the hundreds of tiny wooden parts spread out across the table.

"A B-24 Liberator," he says enthusiastically, handing her the box so she can see what the finished product will look like.

"Cool. So where do we start?"

With Dolo guiding her, Maribel follows his instructions and uses the thin paintbrush to carefully apply glue to each miniature part before placing it in its correct location. It a task requiring much time and patience, but to Maribel's surprise she enjoys the activity, and can tell Dolo does also, despite his role being limited to mainly directing her.

As the weeks pass, she and Shawn spend much of their time at Dolo's place. Maribel and Dolo work on their plane projects together while Shawn watches, plays or naps. Maribel finds herself not only excited about their next model, but also looking forward to the two of them working closely with one another. She anticipates those moments when his hand brushes across hers or when they silently lock eyes and exchange flirtatious smiles. They undoubtedly grow closer and closer, despite her trying to ignore her emotions and resist his charms. But although they spend a great deal of time together, the two do not officially become a couple, due to her fear of another disastrous relationship.

Not that the topic hasn't come up. On many occasions Dolo asks Maribel to be his girlfriend, only to be shot down with the same reply: "I'm just not ready for a relationship, Dolo. You know my past."

Yes, he knows her past. She had told him how she'd been deceived and betrayed by her former lover, Aaron. And he knows that she had lost her best friend Shawna in a car crash caused by a drunk driver. She's been hurt and has lost the only people she ever loved. Dolo understands why Maribel might be a little apprehensive about trusting and loving again, but he has been doing his best to show her that he is different and worth the risk.

On the days they aren't together, he is sure to check up on her to see if there is anything she needs. He is always there for her and Shawn, and treats him as if he was his own son, buying him diapers and unexpected gifts like toys and clothes. He is always a gentleman; he continues to open every door for her, pull out her chair and treat her with kindness and respect at all times. Dolo often wonders if he will be forced to remain in the friend zone forever, but nevertheless, he loves spending time with Maribel and wouldn't give it up for anything.

Maribel truly enjoys the time she spends with Dolo as well, and at times she feels bad about turning him down. She appreciates all that he does for her and Shawn, and she doesn't want him to feel he's being taken advantage of, but she wants to be sure he is genuine before rushing into a relationship. She had been fooled once before by Aaron, and she doesn't want to make the same mistake twice.

After receiving the flowers and money, no more mystery gifts arrive, and Maribel has all but forgotten about them and stopped racking her brain about where they might have come from. But the curiosity and confusion set in all over again when one day she receives another anonymous package at her door. She opens it and inside is a blue Tiffany's jewelry box containing a beautiful white gold necklace with a stunning diamond teardrop pendant. *What the hell is going on?* she wonders. *First the flowers, then $2,500 and now a damn diamond necklace. Who is sending this stuff?* She would soon find out.

Chapter 11

Maribel steps out one evening to get some fried wings from the Chinese store around the corner from her mother's house. It is a walk she is familiar with and she takes her usual route through the driveway located behind the houses on the next block over, and around the corner. The driveway is dark, as most of the bulbs in the lights behind the houses have been broken or burned out, and most of the neighbors have not bothered to change them. But it is a short walk and one she's done countless times over the years to satisfy a late night snack craving.

"Hey, Kim," she greets the aging Asian woman behind the bullet-proof glass. "Let me get three wings with shrimp fried rice and an egg roll. Salt, pepper, ketchup on the wings."

While paying for her food, she hears a car pull up in front of the store. She turns to look through the window, but the car has already sped off. Sticking her head out the store's open door she can see the taillights of the dark vehicle cruising up the street. Kim lets her know her food is ready and Maribel grabs the bag and leaves.

She turns back down the dark driveway and starts to walk through. She thinks she hears footsteps behind her but when she turns she sees no one and the footsteps stop. She continues walking and this time she is sure she hears someone walking behind her but still doesn't see anyone when she turns to look. She ups her pace to a jog, unsure of if someone is really behind her or if it's just her mind playing tricks on her. Either way, she wants to be out of the darkness and under the streetlights where she can be more sure of her surroundings. As she comes to the end of the driveway the black Phantom appears out of nowhere and speeds up onto the sidewalk, blocking her path. Before she has time to think or react, one of the back doors swings open and out steps a ruggedly handsome man with dark, slick hair and a huge smile on his face. He opens his arms and coolly struts towards her.

"Fancyyy! Long time no see, babe."

She squints her eyes tightly and racks her brain trying to figure out where she's seen the stylish, well-dressed man before. From his expensive looking shoes and the cut of his dark gray suit, she can tell he's pretty well-off. But while she knows she recognizes his face as well as his Italian New Yorker accent, she can not, for the life of her, recall from where.

"Who are you?" she asks him. "Where do I know you from?"

"It's me! Tony!"

Tony? she thinks. *Tony...hmmm the name rings a bell.*

"We met at Velvet one night, about a year ago."

She's still unable to recall exactly who he is. She had met many men at Velvet.

"We had a one night stand and you never called me after that."

Shiiiiit. It all starts to come back to her. She had been at Velvet with Brittany and Jaslyn, the same as usual. It was a typical night, for the most part. The three ladies had danced all night and Maribel had consumed more liquor than she could handle. What was different was that she had left the club with a handsome stranger and spent the night with him. The last thing she remembered from the previous night was being in the VIP at the club with her friends. When she woke up naked next to Tony in his bed, she realized she had blacked out and they had slept together. *But what on Earth is he doing here now,* she wonders, looking him up and down suspiciously.

"Why the hell are you here, Tony?" *The flowers...the money...the necklace!* she recalls, realizing they must have been from him. It is all starting to make sense to her. "You're the one who's been sending me all that stuff, aren't you? You've been stalking me!" She begins to feel genuinely afraid and bolts around the car and down the sidewalk.

"Fancy, wait!" he yells, running after her. "Hold up! I'm not gonna hurt you. I just want to be in my son's life!" His words stop Maribel dead in her tracks. She stands there frozen with fear and confusion, trying to internalize what Tony has just said.

"Your son?" she says, whipping around.

47

"*Our* son."

"Are you fuckin' nuts?! You think because you send some money and shit you can just pop up out of the blue claiming my son? I know who his father is, thank you very much!"

"I know this is hard for you to take in right now, but he *is* my son."

"And what makes you so sure?"

"He was born around July 12th right?"

"Yeah, so? And how do you even know that?"

"I saw you on the news, leaving the hospital. They were doing a story about a girl who got murdered at Einstein and you were in the background, walking out with the baby. I recognized you immediately. I did the math and we were together just about nine months before then."

"Tony, you are not the only man I slept with."

"When I saw you walking on Walnut Street, I got a good look at the kid and goddamn it, he looks just like me! He even has the De Luca head."

She studies Tony's face. There are some similarities. Shawn certainly looks more like Tony than Aaron. His skin hue, hair texture and facial features are all a closer match to Tony's.

"Look at me, Fancy!" he hollers at her. "Does he not resemble me?!"

"Stop yelling at me!" she screams, stepping back from him. "He does a little," she admits. "But coincidences happen every day. None of this means anything."

"Think about it, Fancy. It all makes perfect sense."

"So wait," she says, thinking harder about all he's laying on her. "You're telling me we didn't use any protection?"

"No, we didn't."

She is angry and wants to punch him in the face and ask him why he would do something so stupid, but she knows the blame also falls on her. Had she not been so inebriated, she would have been aware of what was going on and could have avoided behaving so recklessly. She realizes she has no one to be mad at but herself and finally accepts that there is a real possibility that Tony is Shawn's father.

"Well I guess it's possible then, but we won't know anything for sure until you take a paternity test."

"Then we'll have to do that ASAP."

Chapter 12

Maribel can not believe it. She had all but forgotten Tony and the night they spent together, so she never considered the possibility that he, or anyone other than Aaron for that matter, could be Shawn's father.

"It's would be a blessing!" Anna exclaims when Maribel tells her about Tony and the conversation they had in the driveway. "If this guy is really Shawn's dad, you won't have to struggle anymore. And now Shawn will have his father in his life."

"But I don't know anything about him! I don't even know if he's the type of man I want around my son, or if he's really even his father for that matter!"

Her answer comes five days later when the DNA test confirms that Tony is, in fact, Shawn's father.

"Yes! I knew it!" he proudly exclaims. "Let me hold my baby boy." After a slight hesitation Maribel hands Shawn to Tony, reminding him to support his head and neck. Tony stares at his infant son in adoration. "That's daddy's little man." Maribel notices the awkward way he handles Shawn. He doesn't seem too experienced with holding a baby.

"You don't have any other children, do you Tony?"

"Nah, just my little bambino."

"Your little what?"

"Bam-bi-no. It's Italian for baby. My pop called me that when I was a baby, too. Wish he could've seen Shawn before he passed. He died a couple weeks ago."

"I'm sorry to hear that."

"Yeah. He was a great man. A real stand up guy. Always was a great father to me and my siblings. And I'm gonna be just as good of a dad to Shawn." He doesn't take his eyes off Shawn as he speaks.

Maribel watches and listens intently, curious to know more about the man that is her son's father, but still a stranger. She thinks he is incredibly handsome; olive skin, a toned body, and jet-black hair with hazel eyes. His slight mustache and goatee lend a rugged edge to his appearance that she finds sexy. But there is no mistaking he is a man with an appetite for the finer things. Just like the last time she saw him, he dons a crisp, tailored suit and handmade Italian leather shoes. *Sharp as a tack*, she thinks. Her eyes work their way from his face to his slightly muscular biceps, flexing through the sleeves of his jacket. She wishes his shirt would magically unbutton itself so she can get a look at what she imagines to be a chiseled chest and abs. Tony finally looks up from Shawn, and Maribel quickly glances away to avoid being caught admiring his physique.

"So how do you feel about all of this, Fancy?"

"Well, um, actually my name is Maribel."

"You gave me a fake name?" he laughs.

"No. I used to go by that name. Everyone called me Fancy. But I started using my real name again so please, call me Maribel."

"I like Fancy better. It fits you more."

"Well I like Maribel. And about you being Shawn's father...I feel...actually kind of relieved. I'm so glad the man I thought was his father really isn't."

"Who'd you think was his pop?"

"That's a looong, crazy story. I'll tell you about it some other time. Anyway, I thought I was gonna be a single mom and have to raise him by myself, but I'm glad he's gonna get to have his dad in his life."

"Damn right, baby," Tony says, holding Shawn close to him with one arm and putting the other around Maribel's waist. "I'm gonna take good care of the both of you."

Maribel shifts uncomfortably. She naïvely hadn't given any thought to the possibility that Tony might also want a relationship with *her*. She can see that he is wealthy; that's apparent by his designer suits and shoes, Breitling watch, diamond encrusted "TD" initial cufflinks and the fact that for the past several weeks he's been stalking her in a chauffeured Rolls Royce. (*Who does that?*) And she recalls waking up in his impressive Center City

52

high-rise apartment and riding in his brand new Mercedes-Benz the morning after their drunken encounter. But up until this point she had completely forgotten that not only had he sent money for the baby; he also sent roses and a diamond necklace for her as well. It dawns on her that Tony plans on buying her affections, and although she undoubtedly would have jumped at the opportunity a year ago, she remembers that everything that glitters isn't gold. Maribel thinks it all seems a little too good to be true, especially with the type of luck she's been having.

She tenses up and removes his arm from around her. "Look, Tony, just because you're Shawn's father doesn't mean you're a good man, and it doesn't mean I want you. We're gonna get to know each other slowly, so pump ya breaks, okay?"

"Whoa!" Tony laughs. "You're one feisty li'l mami, huh? I love it! That's cool though. We can do it your way. But trust me, I'm gonna *make* you love me."

He puts a little too much emphasis on the word "make" for Maribel's liking. She quickly grabs Shawn from Tony's arms and walks off, shaking her head in contempt of his arrogance. *He is going to work my nerves.*

When she gets back from meeting with Tony she dials Dolo. She's been avoiding his calls for the past few days while she awaited the results of the paternity test. She knew if she would have spoken to Dolo she'd have ended up telling him about Tony, but she really didn't want to have that conversation unless it was absolutely necessary. And being as though it has been discovered Tony is Shawn's father, she feels there is no point in hiding the truth from Dolo.

"Hey, Dolo. Sorry I haven't been in touch. I just was dealing with something on my end."

"Everything okay?"

"Yeah, I think so. Well, I found out who's been sending me the stuff."

"Yeah?"

"It's this guy I used to date," she says, bending the truth to avoid being judged. She inhales a deep breath then quickly blurts out, "He took a paternity test and it turns out he's Shawn's father."

The line goes silent for what seems like an eternity. Dolo finally speaks when he realizes Maribel is waiting for him to say something, but the only response he can offer is a dull "Wow."

"Yeah, I know. I was pretty shocked myself."

Then Dolo asks a series of questions all at once: "So, who is this guy?", "How do you feel?", followed by the one question he wants answered most, "What does this mean for you and me?"

"Dolo, there really is no *you and me*." Immediately after the words leave her lips she regrets them, realizing they were somewhat harsh. It was not her intention to hurt his feelings, but the damage has been done. Feeling defeated and not knowing what to say, Dolo makes up a lie about someone calling on his other line and says goodbye to Maribel before hanging up. She considers calling him back to apologize and explain but she doesn't, opting instead to just talk to him tomorrow when he calls.

Chapter 13

The next day is Saturday and when her phone rings, she jumps up to answer it, hoping it is Dolo, but it isn't. It's Tony calling to ask if he can come over and see Shawn. Maribel agrees, figuring it will be a good time to introduce Tony to her mom since she's off from work. As soon as Anna sees him pull up in his spotless money green Maybach, she becomes a fan.

"Mari, look at his car!"

"Which one is it?" she says unexcitedly. "The Rolls?"

"No, some green car. It's beautiful. Unlike anything I've ever seen!"

Maribel peeks through the curtains to have a look. Some of the neighborhood kids are crowded around the car oohing and aahing in amazement, and Tony is showing a few of them the inside of the vehicle. He pulls out a wad of money and gives each of them a $100 bill. The kids go running off down the street yelling excitedly and waving the money proudly as Tony strolls up to the door. Anna rushes to the door and has it open before he even has a chance to knock.

"Hiiii!" she says with a huge grin. "You must be my future son-in-law! Nice to meet you, sweetheart!" She gives him a big hug and kisses him on the cheek, leaving bright pink lipstick on his face.

"That's me! Nice to meet you too, Ms...?"

"Call me Mom!"

"Okay, Mom."

Tony brushes and tugs on his suit jacket to rid it of any wrinkles Anna may have caused when she hugged him. Maribel shakes her head at what she's certain are two of the shallowest individuals on the planet. *I was never as bad as either of them, was I?* she wonders. "I bet Tony would like something to eat, Mom," Maribel says, eager to get rid of Anna.

"Nah, actually I'm—"

"I'm sure he would love to try some of your famous pastillos."

"Oh yeah, sure!" Anna says, hustling into the kitchen. "I'll whip some right up."

Maribel rolls her eyes, embarrassed by her mother's behavior. "Don't mind her, Tony. She suffers from an incurable disease known as *joeness.*"

"It's cool. I'm used to it. I generally have that effect on women."

"I'm surprised you drove here today. Thought you were too scared to come to the 'hood without your driver/bodyguard."

"You crazy? Tony De Luca ain't afraid of any 'hood. This is my city. I can go anywhere in Philly and I'm straight. Now where's my Bambino?"

Maribel points to the playpen in the dining room in which Shawn is napping. "He's been asleep

57

for a while so he should be waking up any minute now."

"Okay. Now why'd you walk off on me like that yesterday, Fancy?" he asks.

"Because you were rude. I didn't like your attitude. And it's Maribel, remember?"

"Sorry, baby. I wasn't trying to get you mad. Shit, I'm trying to get on your good side. All I said is I wanna take care of you and Shawn."

"But Tony, that's the thing. It's fine for you to take care of your son, but as for me...well, you and I are not an item. And I'm not looking to get into a relationship."

"We have a child together, Fancy. Why wouldn't you want to be with your son's father? I want us to be a family and you should want that too."

"But I don't even know you!" Maribel yells, throwing her hands up in aggravation. She takes a deep breath and regains her composure. "Like I said, we're going to take our time and get to know each other. I can't tell what the future will hold, but as of now I am happily single."

"A'ight," Tony says coolly, "That's straight. Can I start by taking you and Shawn to dinner tonight? Not a date...just a grub. Cool?"

Maribel shrugs. "You don't have to cook, Mom," she yells in to Anna. "We've decided to go out to eat."

Chapter 14

"Dolce Vita," Maribel reads the sign aloud as they pull up to the valet area in front of the restaurant.

"Yup. It means 'the sweet life.' I live it every day and I want you and Shawn to live it too."

"I like my life just fine, thank you very much."

"You live in the 'hood and you're on welfare, Fancy," Tony says smugly.

"You are so rude!" Maribel scoffs, in disbelief of his impertinence.

"I'm just saying!" laughs Tony, "It won't be for long, though, now that I'm here."

"Yes, my savior," she says sarcastically, rolling her eyes.

"What happened to your spot in the Piazza, anyway?"

"For your information, I moved back in with my mom to save money," she lies, "for the baby."

"Well you won't have to worry about money anymore. I want you and Shawn to come stay with me."

"Here you go again! You are so damn hard-headed."

When they reach the entrance of Dolce Vita, tuxedoed doormen spring the double doors open and welcome them inside.

"Good evening, Mr. De Luca. Your usual table?"

"You know it, Wally."

The restaurant is beautiful and elegantly decorated with rich cream and golden hues, lace tablecloths, crystal chandeliers and marble bar tops. Maribel has never been to a restaurant as nice as this one.

"*Just a grub*, Tony?" she whispers, elbowing him lightly in his side. "I'm not even dressed right to be here." She looks down at her jeans and Chuck Taylor All-Stars.

"You look fine. Sure your wardrobe could use a little sprucing up but we'll handle that at a later date. Anyway, I come here all the time for dinner – at least twice a week – and I spend enough money in this place for us to wear whatever the hell we want. This is the best place in town to get authentic Italian cuisine. Second only to Mom's home cooking."

Once they are seated at a secluded table in the back, a waiter comes and greets Tony enthusiastically. "Buona sera, Signore De Luca!"

"Hey, Frank. How ya doin'? I'd like ya to meet my son and my girl." Maribel steps on Tony's foot under the table and shoots him an annoyed look.

Biting his bottom lip almost hard enough to draw blood, he forces a mock smile, doing his best to mask his anger. "Not the shoes doll...they're my favorite."

When Maribel notices the waiter holding his hand out for hers she smiles a phony, tight-lipped grin and extends her hand.

"Piacere di conoscerla, Signora," he says, kissing her hand before proceeding to gush over Shawn who just stares back blankly at the stranger.

Tony orders a bottle of Dom Pérignon. "You like that, right?" he asks Maribel, who shakes her head approvingly. "I remember you and your friends were drinking it the night we met." Then he turns back to the waiter and says something in Italian before snatching Maribel's menu as she is attempting to read it.

"What the hell, Tony?!"

"I ordered for you already."

"Huh?"

"Baccalà alla vicentina – the best dish on the menu. And the chef is preparing it special the way I like it. It's great. You'll love it."

Maribel clenches her teeth, fighting the urge to give him a piece of her mind. She takes a big gulp of her water and crosses her arms in agitation. She is glad when the champagne arrives and hopes it will help calm her down.

Shortly after, their entrees arrive and Frank sets them on the table with a "Buon appetito!" Maribel is surprisingly pleased with her creamy codfish dish, even if it was forced upon her.

As they enjoy their dinner, she tells Tony a revised version of the things that occurred in her life over the past year. He seems peeved when she tells him about her run-in with Bella and the Latin Queens, but turns bright red with anger when he hears about the incident with Brittany and Aaron.

"So that news story I saw about the girl that was killed having her baby," that hit was intended for you and Shawn? I'm tellin' ya, it's curtains for that Aaron Jameson dude."

"Yeah, he's rotting in jail."

"That ain't what I meant. Anyway, what happened to the two chicks?"

"Bella was supposed to be doing a nice li'l bid, but I imagine she's out by now, most likely under witness protection. She snitched on the national gang heads and now their offering up some major gwap for her."

"Oh yeah?"

"Yep. And as for Brittany…she's around somewhere. And she better hope she never runs into me. That bitch actually used to call herself my friend. Smiled in my face and turned around and stabbed me right in the back. Anyone plotting against an innocent unborn baby is pure evil and deserves whatever karma throws their way."

"All of 'em deserve to pay," Tony says, shaking his head. "Can't just let that slide." His nostrils flare and his hands ball into fists. "Nobody gets away with trying to bring harm to me and mine."

Maribel can tell that he is as serious as cancer but she forces an awkward laugh, attempting to lighten the mood. "Let me find out you a gangsta'! I sure hope not, 'cause I've had enough drama to last me the rest of my life. I don't need any more craziness around me. But really though, what do you do, Tony?"

"Construction."

"You expect me to believe you ballin' like this on a construction worker's income? I must have the word 'fool' written on my forehead." She looks at her reflection a spoon, rubbing her forehead as if inspecting it for the word.

"Nah, my family owns one of the largest construction companies in the country. I work for the biz, just like everyone else in my family."

"Oh, okay. So basically you were born with a silver spoon in your mouth."

"Trust me, I put in work. I earn every dime I make, and it ain't easy."

"If you say so."

Her words are skeptical but somehow, Maribel believes what Tony says. While he does flirt and joke around with her, he can sometimes be very stern and serious. She can't help but feel that there is something dark lurking inside of him; something about him that just scares her a little. She can see it in his eyes – they turn frigid at times – and while he is physically there with her, it seems that his mind occasionally drifts somewhere far off.

Shawn begins to get fussy so Maribel takes a premade bottle from the diaper bag to feed him. Several minutes into the feeding session Tony says he wants a turn feeding Shawn so she shows him the correct way to hold the bottle to prevent Shawn from swallowing too much air as he drinks. He looks uncomfortable holding Shawn but nevertheless Maribel is glad he is trying and happy that he seems proud to be a father; *a good start*, Maribel thinks. Yet she can't help but notice how much easier Shawn had taken to Dolo. It amazes her how natural Dolo is with Shawn and how Shawn always seems to be watching him and smiling at him. She looks at her phone for the umpteenth time that night to see if she has any texts or missed calls from Dolo, but there are none.

Chapter 15

During the ride home from Dolce Vita, Maribel's phone rings and she digs it out of her bag, hoping it is Dolo. She is slightly disappointed when she sees it is her mother calling; she reluctantly answers the call.

As soon as she answers she hears Anna yelling frantically, "Mari, the house is on fire!"

"What?!" She might have thought Anna was joking if it weren't for the sounds of sirens and chaos in the background. "Are you okay?"

"Yeah. When you guys left I went over to Paula's. I just came home and saw the smoke and fire trucks as I was walking up. I was only gone a little over an hour!"

"Okay, I'm coming now. Be right there."

Nearing the vicinity of her mother's house, Maribel can smell the fire and see the blanket of gray smoke that seems to cover the whole neighborhood; the closer they get, the thicker the smoke becomes. She spots a teary-eyed Anna sitting on the curb across the street from her home, watching helplessly as firefighters battle the blaze consuming it.

"Mom, what happened?"

"I don't know, Mari. I told you I wasn't home."

"Did you leave anything on? The stove? The iron? Curlers?"

"No, of course not. I was wondering if maybe you did."

"I'm positive I didn't. I haven't used any of them in days."

"Well, I spoke to the fire chief and he said sometimes an electrical problem or a defect in a kitchen appliance can cause a fire. They'll do an investigation to find out for sure, but it might take a while. I just can't believe it. I've lost everything in the blink of an eye! Everything I own. Everything I've worked for all these years!"

"Don't you have insurance on the house?"

"I used to, but I stopped paying it a couple years ago. It was too expensive and I couldn't afford to keep up with the payments." Anna starts to cry again and Maribel hugs and consoles her.

"Well don't worry, Mom. Everything will be okay. What's important is that you, me and Shawn are safe. All those material things can be replaced."

"You're right, Mari. As long as I still have you and my little Papito I haven't lost everything."

"Do you have any idea where we can go?"

"I spoke to Daniela and she said we can come stay at her house in Connecticut, but I figured you'd rather for you and Shawn to go to Tony's or Dolo's – some place better."

Anna does have a point. Daniela, her mother's younger sister, is married with five children. They haven't been to Hartford to visit her in about six years. At the time they only had three kids, but the house was a crowded, chaotic mess.

Maribel can only imagine how much crazier it must be now with two additional children.

"There's not even enough room over there for Aunt Daniela and her family. Where are you going to sleep?"

"She says I can stay in the basement for the time being. I'll make it work. On the bright side, at least I get to escape that horrible job. Hell, maybe I'll even find me a decent man out there."

Only my mother can think of finding a man at a time like this, Maribel thinks, in lieu of making the smart remark out loud. While Anna hopes for a new beginning in a new place, Maribel worries about where she and her son will go. Either of her two options sound better than her Aunt Daniela's, yet the idea of having to depend on a man again is somewhat scary. This time she won't even have her mother's house as a safe haven to run back to should something go wrong.

Her initial gut instinct tells her Dolo would be the best choice. He is so kind and good-hearted; a great man, indeed. But she's not even sure Dolo will speak to her again. He seemed really hurt by the comment she made on the phone the previous night and hasn't called all day.

Tony, on the other hand, can certainly be arrogant and crass at times. Yet she considers that maybe she hasn't given him a fair chance. She knows that no one is perfect. Everyone, including her, has faults. Tony seems to have good intentions and to really want to be there for her and Shawn. Plus, he *is* Shawn's father.

She looks toward Tony's car and sees him sitting in the driver's seat smiling at Shawn as he bounces him on his knee. He kisses him on his head and hugs him close. He really loves being a father and is so proud of his little "Bambino." Maribel can't help but smile at the sight of the two of them together.

Having grown up without her father, she always desired to be part of a close-knit family. She considers that maybe this is her chance. Perhaps everything happened for a reason and the whole fiasco with Aaron was meant to occur so she could discover that Tony was Shawn's real father and so they could be reunited. She has to give Tony a chance and give her and Shawn a real shot at having a normal family and a happy life.

She gets back in the car and after closing the door, allows her head to fall back onto the leather headrest, closes her eyes and takes a deep breath to calm her nerves.

"Your mom okay?"

"Yeah, she's gonna go to my aunt's in Connecticut."

"You and Shawn wanna stay with me? I mean you can have your own room and stuff. Whatever you want. I got plenty of space. Just want to make sure you guys are safe."

"Okay."

Tony looks at Maribel with astonishment. "Really? You're gonna come?"

"I'm gonna give it a chance. After all, you are his father."

"Yes, I am. We can pick up some diapers and stuff tonight and in the morning we can go shopping for whatever you and Shawn need. Looks like yous guys are gonna have to start fresh."

"From scratch. We have nothing." A lone tear slides down Maribel's cheek as she watches the smoke rise from the flamed-engulfed blackened structure that was once her home. She had grown up in the house. So many memories were birthed there. It had always been the refuge she could run to when she fell upon hard times and needed a place to stay. And now it is burning to ashes right before her very eyes.

"Don't worry, baby. I got you," Tony says, putting his arm around her shoulders and squeezing her tightly to comfort her. Although Tony is practically a stranger, she finds an odd comfort in his words and is glad he is willing to step up to the plate to help her and Shawn in their hour of need.

Chapter 16

After a lengthy drive through Montgomery County's pitch-black winding lanes and back roads, they arrive at Tony's place, a gorgeous secluded mansion enclosed within large, iron Georgian gates. The house flaunts impressive landscaping, including spiral-shaped shrubs and lawns manicured to perfection. Upon entering the front door, Tony is greeted by a huge, angry-looking man dressed in black, sitting in a chair by the front door. He appears to be in his mid forties and sports a five o'clock shadow and dirty blonde hair along with several noticeable scars, the most prominent being a long, dark scar on the side of his neck. To say he appears to have had a hard life is an understatement. He reeks of cigarette smoke and, from the looks of it, he could really use a haircut and a shave.

"Fancy, this is Bo," Tony begins the introductions. "Bo, this is Fancy and this handsome little solider is my son." Bo's eyes move from Maribel to Shawn and afterwards, he nods a silent greeting. "They'll be staying here from now on." Maribel is unable to take her eyes off of the nasty scar on Bo's neck and finds herself wondering how he managed to get it.

"That one's from a bar fight, believe it or not," he says to her in a scruffy voice that matches his appearance.

"Huh? Oh, I—"

"It's okay, people are always curious about the scars; especially that one. I'm used to it. Yeah, the asshole sliced me good. Tried to take me out, but it's gonna take more than a pussy ass Swiss Army knife to get rid of ol' Bo!" He and Tony laugh hysterically and pat each other on the back.

"Hey, come on now, Bo," Tony says, his tone turning serious. "Watch your fuckin' language around my son."

"Oh, 'scuse me boss," Bo says, apologizing for his use of profanity in front of Shawn. "I gotta get used to the kid being here."

They continue into the house and Tony notices Maribel admiring a row of brushed gold-framed photos on the mantle.

"This here is my ma," he says, pointing to a portrait of an attractive woman with striking features.

"She is beautiful."

Then he points to a snapshot of him and a slightly older man posing with golf clubs on a golf course. "This is me with the Philly Police Commissioner. He's a good friend of the family."

"Oh, I see."

And this is me with the whole fam…well, all the De Lucas that are here in PA at least." He points to a picture of about 30 people sitting at the longest dinner table she's ever seen.

"Wow, your family is huge, Tony."

"Yeah, I guess there are quite a few of us," he laughs. "That's at one of Ma's dinners. It's rare anyone would miss one of those."

"I don't really have any family, aside from my mom and Shawn. I have my mom's sister in Connecticut but I hardly ever see her."

"You don't have any brothers or sisters?"

"Nope. Only child."

"Where's your dad?"

"Who knows? Puerto Rico, probably. I never met him."

"That's a shame. This is my dad," he says, handing her a photo of him and his father.

"I see where you got your style and fashion sense from."

"Yeah. Pa always taught us to dress to command respect. Feels like I was born in a suit."

"This was my best friend," says Maribel, opening the gold heart locket dangling from her neck to show Tony the photo of Shawna she had inserted after her death. "She was the closest thing I had to a sister."

"She?"

"Yeah, she was a bit of a tomboy."

"You named Shawn after her?"

"Yep."

"How come you're not wearing the necklace I got you? I spent a nice chunk of change on that."

"I don't know. I just always wear this one, I guess."

"Well, start wearing it."

They continue through the house and Tony gives Maribel the grand tour. Now she had been really impressed with Aaron's house, but Tony's is twice as large and even more luxurious. With an infinity pool, a huge, ultra-modern kitchen and an actual movie theater, Tony's mansion definitely takes the cake as the most beautiful home she has ever seen. It is the epitome of modern luxury. His "garage" is more of an auto showroom, an all glass building filled with half a dozen luxury vehicles.

The one thing that Maribel finds a little strange is the amount of security Tony has for his home. There are armed men posted at each entrance, Bo being the one stationed at the front door. In addition there is a guard at the front gate and several surveillance cameras around the perimeter. With all the security measures he has taken, it is obvious to her that Tony is either extra cautious or extremely paranoid.

Bruno is the guard stationed at the back door in the kitchen and the sight of him instantly sends chills running down Maribel's spine. While apparently significantly older than Bo, he's just as large in stature, and looks just as rough. It's obvious, however, that he isn't nearly as sociable. The man looks as if he hasn't cracked a smile in decades; a real cold-hearted and no-nonsense type of guy. Bruno sits as still as a lion patiently watching his prey, waiting for the ideal moment to strike. Tony doesn't speak to Bruno or bother to introduce Maribel.

"Does he always sit there like that?" she asks in a hushed tone.

"Yeah, pretty much. He's here every night doing his job. Gone during the day." Maribel is relieved to hear it. She can't imagine cooking breakfast in the kitchen with Bruno's presence and icy stare creating the ultimate awkward and uncomfortable atmosphere.

"Don't worry. I know Bo and Bruno are a little intimidating, but they're on our side. They're here to protect us from anyone who may wanna hurt us." Maribel nods her head, signifying that she understands.

Tony concludes the tour on the second floor, showing Maribel a couple of bedrooms for her and Shawn. "We can have them decorated any way you want."

"Wow, your house is amazing, Tony. But what happened to your apartment in Center City? Got too small for ya?"

"No, I still have it. I used to stay there when I was in the city and didn't feel like coming all the way back here. I'm letting a friend of mine stay there now, though."

Once Shawn is bathed and put down to sleep Tony runs a hot bubble bath for Maribel in the bathroom connected to her room.

"It'll do you good to mellow out and take a load off. I know today was a rough day, but it'll get better – I promise. You're in good hands now."

"Thanks, Tony." She closes the door and slips out of her clothes and into the warm sudsy water as the steam rises all around her. *Ahhhh, this feels great*, she thinks, relaxing deeper into the Jacuzzi, its jets propelling the water to bubble and swirl all around her body. She figures her mother must be halfway to Connecticut by now and she is content knowing she will be with family, while her and Shawn are safe with Tony. If all goes well, maybe the three of them will even be a picture-perfect family of their own.

After her bath, she wraps herself in one of the fluffiest, softest towels she's ever felt, before walking down the hall to Tony's room. She taps gently on the open door, drawing his attention from the crime drama on TV, and asks for one of his T-shirts to sleep in. Tony rises from his king-sized bed and begins rummaging through his dresser drawers, stealing glimpses of Maribel through the mirror every few seconds. He can't manage to keep his eyes off her still-wet body and soon forgets what he is looking for, preoccupied with memories of their one night together. Finally regaining his focus, he stares intently into the drawer to avoid being distracted by Maribel and his lustful thoughts of her. He finds a shirt and as he is handing it to her, he notices a single drop of water running down her neck and chest, disappearing between her perfect breasts.

"Thanks," she startles him out of his daydream.

"No problem."

She turns to leave, but that is the last thing he wants. "Hold up," says Tony, grabbing her by the hand gently. "Why don't you let me give you a massage?"

"A massage, though?" Maribel laughs. "You really think the ol' massage trick's gonna work on me?"

"Nah, seriously. I know you could use one after the day you've had. Plus, I'm famous for my magic hands."

"I bet! They've probably been all over every broad in Philly."

"Nope, only a select few. So consider yourself lucky to receive the offer." Maribel rolls her eyes and smirks, crossing her arms. "But seriously, though…I'll just rub your back for you and then you can go to your room and go to sleep. That's it. I promise to be a gentleman."

"Hmmm," Maribel purrs, considering his offer. "My muscles *are* tight as hell from all the stress. You promise you won't try nothing?"

"Fancy, I cross my heart," Tony says, drawing an imaginary X across his chest with his index finger.

"I don't know why you insist on calling me that," she sighs, lying down on Tony's bed and positioning the towel very carefully so that nothing more than her back is exposed. He takes the massage oil from his nightstand and warms a bit of it up in his hands. Then he proceeds to rub her down, starting with her neck and shoulders, and working his way down her back. He works slowly, using every part of his strong hands, from the fingers to the palms to the heels of his hands. He is attentive and applies just the right amount of pressure. He notices how smooth and soft her skin is and loves how her buttery complexion contrasts against his black sheets. When he reaches the small of her back he is so tempted to tear the towel off of her lovely mounds and ravish her, but he realizes that would only work against his ultimate goal of getting her to trust him. He promised to behave so behave he must.

Once he finishes Maribel just lies there, still as a corpse. He thinks perhaps she has fallen asleep until she finally begins to sit up and re-adjust the towel.

"Damn, you weren't lying about those hands being magic. Thanks, Tony."

"Anytime. Goodnight, Fancy," he says.

"Night."

She exits the bedroom and he watches her walk down the hall and close her bedroom door behind her before retreating back into his bed for the night.

About an hour later Shawn starts to cry and Maribel and Tony meet in the hall as they both rush to console him. She is somewhat surprised he is responding to Shawn's cries but is glad he cares enough to do so. *It'll be a relief to have some help with the baby*, she thinks, watching Tony cradle and shush Shawn. They go downstairs and Maribel shows Tony how to prepare Shawn's bottle then allows him to feed him, burp him, and lay him back down.

"You're really good with him, especially considering you don't have any experience with babies."

"I'm learning."

"I appreciate the effort you're putting into it."

"Of course. That's my son. If there's one thing I learned from my father it's that family comes first."

They walk down the hall to their rooms but neither of them are able to fall back asleep right away. Maribel tiptoes to Tony's room and hearing the television on, she taps on the door.

"Come in," he calls out from the other side.

"I can't sleep. Figured I'd see if you wanted to watch a movie or something." The two watch Natural Born Killers until they both doze off into a deep slumber.

Chapter 17

The next day, Maribel awakens alone in Tony's bed feeling refreshingly well rested. She looks at the stainless steel digital clock on the nightstand and realizes it is a little after one in the afternoon, and by far the latest she's slept since Shawn's birth. She goes into his room to look for him, but he isn't there.

Frantically, she starts down the hallway toward the staircase and as she nears it, the sound of men's voices grow louder and louder. Remembering she is only wearing a T-shirt, she stops in her tracks and instead peeks down the staircase. She breathes a sigh of relief when she see's Shawn sitting safely on Tony's lap, happily sucking down a bottle. She observes Tony and his guests for a moment. They are an odd-looking bunch – all Italian she supposes – and like Tony, they are all wearing suits. Many of the men appear to be substantially older than Tony, leading her to believe they aren't his friends. The men are strewn about on the couches and chairs, comfortably lounging as if they could be family, yet the demanding tone of Tony's voice is all business, suggesting they could possibly be employees of his. But she is unable to catch the gist of their conversation before they become aware of her presence, bringing their talk to a suspiciously abrupt halt.

Tony excuses himself and approaches Maribel, locking eyes with her and nodding his greeting with his trademark bad boy swagger. Holding Shawn in his left arm, he quickly puts his right arm around her waist, ushering her back up the staircase and down the hall. When they are outside of her room, he hands over Shawn before retrieving his wallet from his back pocket.

"What was that about?" she asks, looking toward the stairs. "Who are they?"

"Here," says Tony, as he hands her his American Express Centurion card, ignoring her questions. "Go do some shopping. Get whatever you and Shawn need...anything you want, okay? That's a black card so there's no limit. James is out front when you're ready. He can take yous anywhere ya wanna go. Call me if ya need me." And with that, he hurries back to the living room, leaving Maribel standing there open-mouthed holding his credit card and their son.

Maribel tells the driver, James, to take her and Shawn to the nearest mall. She buys several outfits for the two of them, a couple pairs of shoes, and some essential items like underclothes. Regardless of his instructions, she doesn't want to take advantage and spend too much of Tony's money. But when she comes back into the house with only four shopping bags, he looks at her as if she has two heads.

"That's all you got?"

"I just got a few things to get us started."

"Fancy, I give you a black card and tell you to get whatever you want and you go to the strip mall and come back with four bags?" he asks, confused. "Let me see what you got." She begins to pull some of the clothing out of the bag and Tony inspects it quickly. "What the fuck is this shit? I don't work as hard as I do for my woman and my son to be walking around here dressing like average people."

"Tony, I am not your woman. And you're talking like you're some celebrity."

"Listen, while you stay under my roof, you are my woman, and I'm taking care of you. I'm Tony De Luca and you represent me. Ain't no woman of mine shopping at no fuckin' JC Penney. What's this bullshit you bought my son?" Tony throws the bags across the couch and heads for the door. "Let's go."

They get in Tony's Range Rover and head toward I-95N.

"Where are we going?" Maribel asks.

"New York."

Tony takes Maribel on a shopping spree up and down 5th Avenue, hitting only top of the line designer stores: Louis Vuitton, Saks and Bergdorf's before dinner; Gucci, Pucci, Prada and Escada after. They shop for entire new wardrobes for her and Shawn. There's no questioning, looking at price tags or trying anything on. Tony buys whatever Maribel wants. He also personally selects various items for her and Shawn, and even takes the liberty of putting together several outfits for them, all to suit his liking, of course. Sure, she finds his styling them a little strange, but Maribel doesn't object since Tony is paying for it all on his limitless credit card. After all, she reasons, there's no harm in rocking the latest designer fashions – if you can afford it. And Tony has made it very clear that he can not only afford to spoil her and Shawn, but that he *wants* to do so. Maribel had never owned so many designer clothes, shoes and handbags in all of her "Fancy" years combined, and finds it ironic how she was never able to have all that she desired until now, when she's no longer pressed to have it.

They stay in New York shopping for hours until there is no more room in the truck for any more bags.

Chapter 18

Within days Maribel finds herself falling comfortably into the lifestyle Tony is providing for her and Shawn. He spoils them, showering them with gifts, attention and affection. Many nights they dine at Dolce Vita, but she equally enjoys the evenings they spend at home with her home-cooked meals or cuddled up with a movie. She continues sleeping in her own separate bedroom, and Tony is patient about not rushing the romance and allowing things to progress at Maribel's pace.

One afternoon Tony surprises her with tickets to a Phillies game.

"Ooooh, fun!" she squeals. "Never been to a Phillies game before."

"Are you kiddin' me? You're gonna love it. My pop used to take us as kids."

Their seats are among the best in the stadium. They are front and center of all the action eating popcorn and drinking soda. Tony is very into the game. When he's not cheering or jeering he's talking to Shawn, attempting to explain to him the ins and outs of baseball, and what is happening in the game.

"You see, Shawn, the batter just struck out, meaning he missed three times. And that's a good thing for us, because he's not on our team."

Maribel laughs, as Shawn looks up at the darkening sky, oblivious to the game and all that

Tony is saying. Then she glances quickly at the Jumbotron and does a double take when she notices her, Tony and Shawn are on the screen.

"Look, Shawn!" she says, trying to get the baby to direct his attention to the huge screen.

"Hey, look...it's us," says Tony. "We make a good-looking family, don't ya think?" Maribel has to agree. They look like the perfect happy family.

Then over the PA system they hear the announcer say, "Hey, it's Tony De Luca! Enjoying the game with a lucky lady."

Tony looks surprised and irritated as his eyes shift from side to side and he forces a nervous wave.

"Wow. You come to games that often? You're like a celebrity here, huh?"

"No, I...I'm friends with the announcer. That's all."

Maribel feels all eyes on them as they leave the stadium after the game. She's been getting accustomed to the feeling. Their aura is one of wealth and class and it's not every day people see such a beautiful family out dressed to the nines. They certainly look like celebrities so it's expected that people will stare.

After the game they head down Oregon Avenue to a place Tony claims has "the best homemade Italian ice in the city." They sit outside at the wooden picnic tables to eat their water ice in the cool late August breeze.

"This is really good," Maribel says, sucking

on a huge chunk of cherry from her water ice.

"I told ya."

"Let me guess. You used to come here when you were little?"

"Yup, all the time. It's cool I get to do all this stuff with Shawn that I used to do with my pop."

"You really wanna be like him, huh?"

"They're some big shoes to fill. For a long time I wasn't sure if I could do it...you know, be like him. I'm not perfect. I have a lot of flaws and a lot of issues. I'm battling demons, Fancy – big ones. I just wasn't sure if I was father material. I've been trying, though. Since you guys been with me, I've been working hard at being more patient, more understanding, and controlling my anger. You and Shawn make me feel like I'm complete...like I can do this. I feel like I'm where I'm supposed to be now and everything just finally feels right."

"I understand, Tony. I have to admit I am enjoying this new family life. I agree with what you said about it feeling right. I'm a little bit scared, though."

"Of what?"

"Just seems too good to be true...that's all. I feel like soon I'm gonna wake up and find that this was all a dream."

Tony pinches her arm.

"Ow, Tony!"

"You're awake."

During the ride home Maribel stares out the window in silence, thinking about Dolo. Although she hasn't spoken him in a week and a half, he has been a permanent fixture in her mind ever since their last phone convo that ended on a sour note. She misses him a lot, and wonders if she should reach out to him.

She eventually drifts off to sleep. When she wakes up she is in Tony's arms and he is lying her down in his bed. She looks around sleepily for her son.

"Where's Shawn?" she yawns.

"In his room sleeping."

"Why'd you bring me to your bed?"

"Because that's where I want you." Tony climbs on top of Maribel and kisses her firmly, immediately silencing her questioning. He moves his wet lips down to her neck, using them in conjunction with his tongue to kiss and lick her seductively, quickly erasing any thoughts she had of leaving his bed. Her mind, in fact, wanders back to her kiss with Dolo, and as Tony's mouth explores her body, she imagines it is Dolo's instead. Tony's tongue and lips continue to work their way down her body, getting reacquainted with her hardened nipples and the smooth skin on her stomach. His lips are no longer the only things wet now. By the time he removes her panties they are soaked and her body is readily anticipating receiving his sizeable package. His left hand reaches into the nightstand drawer, fishing around amongst the guns and bullets, for a condom while his right hand carefully teases her throbbing clitoris. She ignores the clanking the firearms make as they are pushed around in the drawer, but makes a mental note to check out his small armory later. After outfitting his soldier with a Magnum he inserts himself all at once and begins to thrust – hard. He puts her legs back as far as they will go and pumps away like a jackhammer. Maribel is not used to someone being so aggressive. Usually a man will start off slow and gentle and work up to the fast and rough, but not Tony. After a while, and much to her surprise, she finds herself enjoying it more and more. It is somewhat painful, but much more pleasurable. She throws one leg in front of Tony to join her other leg on the opposite of his body and rolls over onto all fours. She arches her back and Tony pushes her head down onto the bed. He pumps harder and harder and Maribel can feel him deep in her stomach. Just as she is about to climax, Tony does so first, collapsing over onto her back, sweating and panting heavily like a thirsty dog. She rolls her eyes and shakes her head at his selfish and inadequate performance.

"I see I'll be needing a vibrator," she mumbles as he makes his way to the bathroom.

"What's that you say?"

"Nothing."

He closes the bathroom door and she sulks, unsatisfied, to her room. "Guess I'll just have to handle it myself," she says once alone in her bed.

She begins to rub and stroke herself, prompting the juices of her creamy center to flow once more. She inserts her middle finger deep inside and swirls it around before adding her index finger and beginning a steady in and out motion that brings her dangerously close to the peak. But her bliss is interrupted by Tony bursting through the door.

"So, I was thinking," he says, strutting over to her bed in his boxers, oblivious to the fact that he just ruined her delightful self-pleasuring. "We ought to change Shawn's name." Maribel is sure this has to be some kind of joke. And right now she is not in the mood for Tony or any of his nonsense.

"That is not an option. Thank you for the visit and goodnight." She turns her back to him and pulls the covers over her head.

"Don't turn your back on me, Fancy. I'm talking to you. You can sleep when we're done discussing this."

"Discussing what?" she yells, jumping up out of the bed and storming towards the bathroom. "As far am I'm concerned there's nothing to talk about. I am *not* changing my son's name!"

Tony steps into her space, blocking her path and putting his face directly in front of hers. "What's with the 'my son' bullshit? He's my fucking son too! Don't you disrespect me by referring to him as only *your* son like I'm some type of deadbeat sperm donor that don't do shit for him!"

"Tony I didn't say you were a deadbeat and I didn't mean anything by it. But I was trying to go to sleep and you just burst up in here talking some old bullshit about changing Shawn's name."

"It's not bullshit! My father was Antonio De Luca, Sr., I am Antonio De Luca, Jr. and I want my son to be Antonio De Luca, III. He should be named after his father, instead of being named after some dead dike bitch!"

"FUCK your father, Tony! And FUCK YOU!"

He backhands her across her face, sending her head whipping around fiercely. Stunned, she grabs her stinging cheek and backs away from him fearfully, until she finds herself boxed into a corner of the room. This is the first time Tony has put his hands on Maribel. She knew there was something dark lurking within him but she never imagined he would ever behave so violently toward her. She realizes she has grossly misjudged his character.

She quivers with fear as Tony slowly makes his way over to the corner. He wraps his fingers around the gold locket and looks at it pensively for a moment before yanking it from her neck, breaking the gold chain in the process. "Don't you EVER talk about my father like that again!" And with that he storms out of the bedroom, slamming the door behind him.

Maribel slides down to the floor, crying quietly. She brings her knees to her chest and wraps her arms around them, rocking back and forth still shocked that Tony just put his hands on her. *He hit me. He actually hit me.*

Chapter 19

Maribel is cooking herself breakfast the following morning when Tony walks into the kitchen. He kisses Shawn good morning before walking over to Maribel, who is standing at the stove making an omelet. He tries to move her hair from in front of her face, to get a look at her cheek but she backs away from him.

"Don't touch me," she says coldly.

"Look Fancy, I'm sorry."

"Uh-huh."

"You were out of line but I handled it wrong. I shouldn't have hit you. It was just a natural reaction. You shouldn't have said that about my pop."

"Well you shouldn't have said what you said about my friend. You know how close I was to her and that was some fucked up shit to say."

"I'm sorry, okay?"

"No, Tony. It's not okay! You *hit* me! I would have never agreed to give you a chance if I knew you were abusive. I can't stay here anymore. Me and Shawn are leaving today."

"Come here, baby." Tony tries to hug her but she pushes his arms away. He is persistent and after several more attempts she stops resisting and allows him to wrap his arms around her, but she stands there as stiff as a board, refusing to look him in the eye or return the embrace.

"Listen to me, Fancy. Please trust me. I am not abusive. I never hit a woman before, and I'll never hit you again. I promise. I love you." His voice cracks as if he will begin to cry at any moment, and he kisses her sweetly on her bruised cheek. "Forgive me, baby...please." She finally looks him in the face and he knows he's got her now. "Please," he pleads. His expression is one of sadness and regret.

She finally relaxes her tightened muscles and hugs him back, laying her head on his shoulder and burying her face in his neck to hold back the tears.

Moments later Tony reaches into his pocket and pulls out a necklace. He places it around Maribel's neck and fastens the clasp.

"Thank you," Maribel says, relieved to have her locket back safely around her neck. But when she touches it she realizes it isn't the locket. Instead, Tony has adorned her neck with the necklace he had bought for her – the one with the diamond teardrop pendant.

"This necklace is beautiful Tony," she says, "but I would like my locket back. It's very special to me, as you know."

"I'm gonna give it back. I just want to have the chain repaired first."

Later that evening Tony goes to Dolce Vita for a business dinner meeting, leaving Maribel and Shawn at home. But Maribel doesn't mind at all. On the contrary she is happy to have the time to herself.

The first thing she does is call to check up on her mother.

"Where's my grandson?" Anna demands. "Put me on speaker so I can talk to him."

"He can hear you."

"Hiiii Shawny-Pooh!" she squeals, annoyingly. How's Abuela's little papito? I missssss youuuuu!"

"We miss you too. So how you liking it out Connecticut, Mom?"

"Well, the living quarters could definitely be better. Daniela's basement is full of junk and has these humongous hairy spiders. Luckily it should only be a temporary arrangement. I met a great guy. He's a marketing executive and if everything goes as planned he'll be asking me to move in with him any day now."

"You don't waste no time, do you Mom?" Maribel chuckles.

"How's Tony? You fall head over heels in love with him yet?"

"He's okay. And for a moment I actually thought I might fall for him, but no, I have not. And I doubt I will."

"I don't understand why you sound so sad, Mari. He's rich, handsome and I'm sure he's taking excellent care of you and Shawn. Any woman would love to be in your shoes."

"Things aren't always as great at they seem."

"What do you mean?"

"Nothing, Mom. But you know, to be honest, I really miss Dolo. I've been thinking about him a lot."

"Aw, I know, Mari. Dolo is a really nice guy. But he can't give you the life Tony can. You can't keep talking to him and risk ruining things with Tony."

"I actually haven't spoken to him in days, but I think I'm gonna call him."

"Be smart now. Shawn needs his father. Don't lose him because you want to think with your heart instead of with your brain."

"Can we change the subject, please?"

"Well fine, but I'm just trying to give you some sound advice. Whether you take it or leave it is ultimately up to you."

"Yada, yada, yada...moving right along. Anyway I wanted to tell you I've been putting a lot of thought into going back to school."

"For what, Mari?! You'll never have to work a day in your life once you marry Tony."

Maribel sucks her teeth. "Oh never mind, Mom. I'm hanging up now."

"Wait a minute! I'm not done talking to you. Someone from the fire marshal's office called me earlier."

"Yeah? What did they say?"

"He said the fire looked like an arson."

"What? You mean they think someone started it intentionally? That's impossible. Who would want to set our house on fire?"

"I know, that's the same thing I said. I think they just have so many open cases that they do a half-assed rush job sometimes. Probably even make shit up just to close cases."

"Yeah, especially in the 'hood. Now I bet ya if we were up in the county somewhere they'd be real thorough about it and do things right."

"Exactly. It was obviously an accident."

Maribel's other line beeps and she sees that it is Trinity calling. "A'ight, well I'll talk to you later, Mom. Just wanted to check up to you."

"Okay. Later, Mari."

"What's up, Trin?" she greets her friend after hanging up with Anna.

"I am good, life is grand and it just got better for you."

"And why, pray tell, is that?"

"Because ding dong, mothafucka! The wicked witch is dead!"

"And that would be...?"

"Bella. Duhhh."

"Damn, for real?"

"Yup. They found her ass in the Schuylkill River, girl."

"Oh shit, that's crazy."

"Ummm-hmmm. Somebody sittin' on some major extra bread right now."

"Damn, they weren't playin'. Well a'ight, Trin. Thanks for the update. I'ma holla at you lata, k?"

"Okay, girl...one."

The news of Bella's death doesn't come as much of a shock to Maribel. She knew it was probable the gang would get a hold of her sooner or later, considering there was a large sum of money being offered for her. She feels a tinge of guilt after realizing the news was sort of a relief to her – a weight lifted. She is free to live without constantly looking over her shoulder and wondering if Bella will be coming after her for revenge.

With Tony out of the house for the evening Maribel takes the opportunity to snoop through his room. After Shawn is fed and dozes off for a nap, her first stop is the top drawer of Tony's nightstand, where he keeps several handguns. Looking past the Heckler & Koch, Glock and Beretta, she is instantly drawn to the gleaming Smith and Wesson .357. It is identical to the one she shot the time Aaron took her to the firing range, except that Tony's is gold instead of silver. She picks it up for a moment, briefly getting reacquainted with the feeling of holding the firearm. Feeling its familiar weight and smooth surface, prompts her to recall the correct form and stance Aaron taught her. Holding the gun at eye level to look down its sights, she takes aim at her reflection in the mirror. *Pow*, she whispers, jerking the gun as she pretends to let off a shot. She places the gun back next to the others and slides the drawer closed.

The second drawer in the nightstand contains mostly papers; receipts, bills, old travel itineraries – nothing of interest – until she digs deeper and comes across several X-rated photos of Tony in compromising positions with various women. Along with the photos, Maribel finds a couple pairs of ladies' underwear. Judging from the fact that the red lace La Perla thong is a size medium while the hot pink Victoria's Secret G-string is an extra-small, she assumes they are from different women.

"Either he's extremely sentimental, saving mementos from his exes," Maribel says to herself, "or somebody's got a couple side chicks."

When Tony comes home from Dolce Vita he has a take-out bag for her containing the codfish dinner she fell in love with the first time he took her there. She experiences the burning urge to question Tony about the lingerie and the women in the photos. But if she asks him about them, he will know she had been snooping in his room and going through his things. And that is not something she believes he will take too kindly to, especially given his apparent bad temper. She decides she will just have to let it go for now. She thanks him for bringing her the food and graciously kisses him on the cheek for the thoughtful gesture.

"So what'd yous guys do while Daddy was out?" he asks, removing his navy blazer and scooping Shawn up in his arms.

"Nothing much. Watched a little Nick Jr., read some books, played with toys…the usual."

"That's good. You miss me, babe?"

"Yup," Maribel lies.

"You better. You okay, though? Seems like you got something on your mind."

"Well…I kinda do. I've been thinking a lot lately about something I've been wanting to do."

"What is it? Spit it out already."

"After we met at Velvet I started going to CCP. I was working on my nursing degree. But when I got pregnant with Shawn I dropped out. Not just like that, though. I mean at first I was just sick a lot and I didn't realize I was pregnant. But I had missed so many days and fell so far behind on the syllabus that I got discouraged. Then when I found out I was pregnant I told Aaron and he didn't want anything to do with me or the baby. I was really depressed after that, which was another reason I never went back to school."

"And you're telling me all this to say…?"

"I want to go back to school and finish getting my degree."

"For what, Fancy?"

"Because it's something I want to do for me, Tony."

"Well, I'm sorry but it ain't happening. There's no point, anyway. I don't see why a woman would want to work if she didn't have to. My pop never let my ma work. He was the provider like a man is supposed to be. My mom's only job was to raise us. And that's all *you* gotta do. Stay home and raise Shawn. That's your job."

"Geez, I would think you'd be happy to have a woman that wants to contribute financially."

Tony can't help but to laugh. "I don't need your li'l contribution, baby. I could earn a nurse's entire yearly salary in a day. Now don't you think this little guy is sleepy? It's late for him to still be up."

Maribel takes Shawn from Tony and after giving him a warm bath, rocks him to sleep and lays him down in his crib. She then goes straight to her room and gets in her bed. She doesn't feel like dealing with Tony anymore tonight. He has put a sour taste in her mouth with his comments about her not needing to work, not to mention the lingerie and photos she found in his nightstand earlier in the day.

Chapter 20

"Oh, Dolo," Maribel moans loudly, her legs quivering with each precise flick his tongue makes on her swollen clitoris. "That feels so good, papi...don't stop." She gyrates her hips and caresses the back of his head, pulling it closer into her. "Yeah, just like that. I'm about to...oooooh, baby, yes...you're gonna make me...mmmmm! Yes...YES! I'm CUMMING!"

Maribel springs up in bed, startled by her own moans and the delightful sensation below. Realizing she just had a wet dream about Dolo, she gets out of bed to change into some dry panties.

"This shit is crazy," she says to herself, removing her moistened underwear and wiping herself dry. She realizes she needs to close the book on the Dolo chapter in order to move on with her new life. She hasn't stopped thinking about him the whole time she's been at Tony's, and can no longer deny her feelings nor her attraction to him.

She wants to tell him that she had not intended to hurt his feelings. She wants to tell him about the way he's been invading her thoughts day and night. She wants to tell her that she loves him. But she won't say any of that. All she plans to tell him is that they can no longer be friends. Her and Shawn will be staying with Tony now and that is that. It's what's best for everyone. Shawn will grow up with his father and they'll never have to want for anything ever again. Yes, she must see Dolo as soon as possible to get the closure she needs and to finally dead the situation and move on once and for all.

Her chance comes two days later when Tony says he wants to take Shawn to his mother's to meet his family. At first she is preparing to leave with them, but Tony says he would rather introduce her separately at a later time since they'll already be in shock about him springing a baby on them. His rationale doesn't make much sense to her, but she doesn't bother arguing once she realizes it will be an opportune time to go talk to Dolo.

Maribel taps lightly on Dolo's front door and nervously waits for it to open. He answers the door wearing a heather gray tee and faded blue jeans with black and gray Jordans. Her heartbeat quickens when she sees him flash his classic winning smile and she has to bite her bottom lip to prevent smiling back at him.

"Hi," he says, noticing her awkward vibe.

"Hello."

"How did you get here?" Maribel turns and looks at the Rolls Royce waiting at the curb with its driver leaning against it, smoking a cigarette.

"Oh. Shawn's father must be pretty well-off then, I guess."

"Are you going to let me in or what, Dolo?"

"Of course. Come on in." She has a seat on his couch while he pours them each a glass of

Chardonnay. She takes a long, slow swig of the wine hoping it will help calm her shaky nerves.

"How's your hand? I see the cast is off."

"It's still stiff but feeling much better. It's getting there."

"I'm surprised you never called me back," she says. "It's been like two and a half weeks."

"You've been counting, huh? Yes, I'm aware that absence makes the heart grow fonder."

"Well anyway, I didn't mean anything by what I said. I wasn't trying to hurt your feelings or anything."

"Ah, don't mention it. It's water under the bridge. What's been up, though? How are you and Shawn doing?"

"We're good. We moved in with his dad," Maribel said, getting to the point of her visit.

"Oh," says Dolo, trying to hide his disappointment. "How's that working out?"

"Great! Shawn really likes him," she lies, with faked enthusiasm.

"And what about you?"

"Huh?"

"Do you love him?" The question catches her off guard and she quickly brushes it off.

"I just came here to tell you that we can't be friends anymore. I think it would be best for everyone."

Dolo doesn't move or blink. He just sits there next to her, reclined on the couch with his arms crossed and matter-of-factly says, "That isn't what you want."

"Yes it is, Dolo."

"Do you think you can truly be happy with a man you don't love?"

"I never said I didn't love him!"

"You never said that you did.

"Why are you so worried about it?"

"I just don't want to see you make a mistake you'll later regret. You don't love him. And you've never told me how you feel about me, but you don't need to. I felt it when we kissed."

"Felt what, Dolo? You—"

Before she can finish her sentence his lips are pressed against hers. The butterflies instantly return to her stomach, fluttering wildly, weakening her and making her feel as if she will melt right then and there. The move was so unexpected and while her mind is thinking about pulling away from him, her body has already given in. Their tongues dance a passionate tango, moving slow and then quick – quick and then slow. They remove each other's shirts and she runs her manicured fingers along his rock hard chest and washboard abs. He lifts her body up in his strong, muscular arms and she wraps her legs around his torso. Dolo carries Maribel up the stairs, his mouth never leaving her body for more than an instant. He lays her gently on his bed and slides off her Stella McCartney harem pants and black lace panties all at once before removing his own jeans. He plants a trail of soft, sensual kisses from her neck all the way down to her freshly shaven kitty and she purrs with delight. Maribel gasps at the first sensation of his tongue on her pink pearl. He is incredibly skilled with his tongue, pleasing and teasing her thoroughly, and knowing just what to do to drive her wild. It is her wet dream come true – only better. When she reaches her peak he inserts his tongue into her honey hole, devouring her delectable nectar like a thirsty hummingbird feeding on morning lily dew. But Maribel knows he isn't done with her yet – he is only getting started. He unleashes his Mandingo warrior and after suiting it in latex armor she guides him inside, happy to receive him. His great length and girth prove to be a perfect fit, as if it were custom molded specifically for her. Each rhythmic stroke sends intense pleasure radiating through her body and she climaxes for a second and third time before he does.

Afterwards they lie on their backs next to each other, staring up at the ceiling as they catch their breath and allow their temperatures and heart rates to return to normal. Thinking about what Dolo had said earlier she knows he is right. She is in love with him. No matter how much she tries to deny it, the truth is she loves everything about him. From his gorgeous smooth skin to his soft, kissable lips. From the kindness he shows her to the rough, no-nonsense side of him. The way he is always a complete gentleman and treats her like a queen. And now, the way he has made love to her in a way she's never experienced before. Maribel knows there is no getting Dolo out of her system now and that things will undoubtedly become much more complicated with her trying to juggle both him and Tony at the same time. She decides not to dwell on her problems. She'll worry about it later. For now she will live for the moment and enjoy being in the arms of the man that she loves. She curls up next to him and lies on his chest, listening to his heartbeat until they both drift off into a deep slumber.

When Maribel wakes up three hours later and realizes she is still in Dolo's bed, she nearly jumps a mile. She scurries frantically around the house, gathering her clothes and throwing them on.

"What's wrong?" Dolo asks. "Everything okay?"

"We've been asleep for three hours!"

"So?"

"I have to go home! James probably left by now and what am I gonna tell Tony?"

"James?"

"The driver!"

Dolo wants to ask her how she could possibly go back to Tony. He can't understand why she wouldn't want to be with him, knowing how they feel for each other. But he doesn't want to sound like a broken record, so he bites his tongue. He looks out the window and sees that the car is still there, parked in the same spot as before.

"Your car didn't leave," he says somberly. "Go ahead before you get in trouble." Maribel is so busy trying to tame her messy hair, she doesn't even notice his changed tone. She quickly pecks him on the cheek and rushes towards the stairs, but once she reaches the staircase she turns around and calmly walks back over to him.

"Dolo?"

"Yes, Love?" he says pulling her body closer to his.

"I love you."

"I know you do, Maribel. And I love you too."

"We'll figure this out. Just bear with me."

"I'm here. I'm not going anywhere."

This time she gives him the kind of good-bye kiss she knows he deserves – a slow, lingering one – before disappearing down the stairs and out the door.

James is on his phone and quickly hangs up when he sees her approaching the car. Maribel is afraid it was Tony on the other end of the call, inquiring about her whereabouts.

"Sorry about that, James. I was so tired I accidentally fell asleep! Why didn't you knock on the door?"

"I just drive the car ma'am. My job is to take you wherever you want to go and then take you home afterwards, no matter where or how long."

"Oh, I see."

Maribel is satisfied with his response and relieved that she will not be in hot water with Tony.

Chapter 21

After getting a taste of what Dolo has to offer, Maribel can't get enough. She sees him every chance she gets and begins having James drop her off at Trinity's and from there having Trinity drop her off at Dolo's. After all, she reasons, James *is* Tony's employee, and no matter what he says, his loyalty still resides with Tony. Using Trinity doesn't come without a price, though. In turn she must be willing to hang out and club with her when she asks. Since she wants to stay in Trinity's good graces to keep her in pocket for when she wants to see Dolo, Maribel obliges.

She soon finds herself falling back into the party lifestyle and getting reacquainted with the drinking and late nights that come along with it. She vows it is only a temporary thing – a sacrifice she must make if she wants to be able to keep up her affair with Dolo – but a couple of weeks soon turn into months, and a few girls nights out turn into a regular weekend ritual.

One Saturday night Trinity tells Maribel she wants to go to Velvet.

"Ugh, why there?" Maribel groans. "Why can't we just go to Plush again?"

"I'm tired of Plush, girl! We went there last weekend and the one before that. What you got against Velvet anyway?"

"Nothing," Maribel says, not wanting to discuss it any further. Despite the bad memories she has of Velvet, she reluctantly agrees to go to her old hangout spot, but only because she wants to spend the night at Dolo's; she tells Tony she's staying at Trinity's.

"Don't you think the clubbing thing is gettin' a little out of hand?" he asks in response. "You go out every weekend. I haven't even met this Trinity broad you're running around with and now you wanna stay at her house overnight? For what?"

"What do you mean? I don't say anything when you go to Dolce Vita for your dinner meetings and wherever else it is you go."

"When I go out I'm handling business...making money...working."

"Well I work too. I'm the one who takes care of our son all day, remember?"

"Yes, and you're a good mom. That's why I don't mind you going out every once in a while. But every weekend? Staying out all night? You're out there running the streets like you ain't got a man at home."

Maribel sighs and smiles, preparing to diffuse the situation. "You're right, Tony. After tonight, I will lay off the partying, okay?" she kisses him goodbye before setting off for the night.

She feels tense preparing to walk into Velvet for the first time in almost a year. She doesn't recognize the bouncer at the door so she slips him an extra $100 to let them bypass the long line outside the club. The place is pretty much the same as the last time she went; crowded with music blaring and strobe lights flashing. Many of the staff and bartenders are new, but she sees a few familiar faces including her favorite bouncer, an Irishman whose name she can't recall. She approaches him, hoping he remembers her and is relieved when his face lights up with recognition.

"Fancy!" he exclaims, opening his arms wide for a big hug. "Where ya been, babe? We haven't seen you in ages."

"I know, right? I had a baby, so I kinda fell back on the clubbing and all."

"A baby? Well damn, you still look great! I would've never guessed you had a child."

"Thanks."

"Your girls still come here sometimes." Maribel's rolling eyes let him know that Brittany and Jaslyn are no longer her girls. "Enough about them, though. Who's this fox you've got with you?"

"This is my friend, Trinity."

They exchange greetings and Maribel and Trinity continue to VIP where they are set up with a bottle of Ciroc. A couple former acquaintances come to say hello and attempt to strike up conversations but she quickly brushes them off. She knows they're not really as concerned or as glad to see her as they pretend; they just want to be nosey, and the last thing she needs is any of them in her business. But for the most part, all is well. The vodka has them feeling good and they are enjoying dancing and letting loose. Trinity is racking up on phone numbers, and Maribel is looking forward to seeing Dolo afterwards. She is flirting with him via text when she glances up from her phone and spots Brittany and Jaslyn walking into VIP. Seeing red, and feeling extra bold from the alcohol, Maribel jumps up without a second thought. When Brittany notices her coming toward her, she quickly grabs Jaslyn's hand and turns to bolt back through the crowd toward the exit.

"Where you going?" Trinity asks, running up behind Maribel.

"That bitch Brittany is here!" she yells over the music, securing her hair into a tight bun with an elastic hair tie.

"Where she at? I got ya back!"

Maribel continues working through the crowd, thinking about her baby boy and what could have happened if Aaron and Brittany's plan had panned out. Brittany is halfway to the door and she simply can't let her get away.

"I *have* to catch her!" Maribel screams desperately. Just the thought of Brittany slipping out of the club unharmed is enough to boost her anger and aggression to level ten. Her adrenaline pumps and her strength turns Herculean. "MOVE!" she growls, pushing club patrons aside.

"Get the fuck out the way!" Trinity backs her up.

When, at last, Brittany's bleach blonde hair is within arms reach she grabs a handful of it and yanks it with all her might, causing Brittany to fall backwards onto the club floor. She violently kicks and stomps Brittany's head and stomach repeatedly.

When Jaslyn tries to pull Maribel off of her friend, Trinity pushes her out of the way and hits her with a few good jabs to the face. Jaslyn, not being a fighter, quickly picks up her purse and scurries out of the club, leaving Brittany to fend for herself.

By the time Trinity turns back to Maribel she's standing over Brittany with her foot on her neck. Brittany's face is a bloody mess and she has no more struggle left in her. In fact, she looks as if she will pass out at any moment from the pressure of Maribel's body weight being exerted directly onto her windpipe by the size seven Zanotti pump.

"Look at you! Maribel scoffs at Brittany, disgusted by the very sight of her. "Not so bad now, are ya Brit?!" She throws her head back and laughs sadistically, putting on a show for all the spectators. "This is for me!" she says, delivering the hardest kick she can muster to the side of Brittany's head. "And this is for my son!" She raises her foot high, preparing to give Brittany's face one final stomp, and all the onlookers brace themselves for the impact the stiletto heel will make when it meets her flesh. But before Maribel's foot lands, the Irishman sweeps her up. Satisfied with the gory new makeover she's given Brittany, she doesn't bother to resist, and she wisely follows his advice to leave before the police arrive.

The ride to Dolo's house is a silent one. Trinity pays close attention to her driving, trying not to let the alcohol in her system alter it, while Maribel uses McDonald's napkins and hand sanitizer to clean the spatters of Brittany's blood off her ankles and shoes.

They pull up outside of Dolo's and Maribel combs her hair and touches up her lipstick in the mirror as she prepares to greet her lover.

"Thanks for having my back tonight, Trin."

"Come on now, what you thought? I gotta say, though...I never would've thought you had that in you."

"Had what in me?"

"I don't know, man. I just saw another side of you tonight. When you had Brittany down on the floor...the look in your eyes. It was like something dark overcame you."

Maribel laughs. "You know I'd been waitin' to run into that bitch. She had it coming."

"I know. I'm not saying she didn't deserve it, but you were like...I don't know...you looked evil as hell. It was like the regular Maribel stepped out and this bad-ass, devilish Maribel took over."

Maribel is unable to control her laughter despite a straight-faced Trinity staring back at her. "Girl, I can't with you tonight. I'ma just ignore your crazy ass 'cause I know that's the Ciroc talking! That bitch was tryna' help Aaron get me killed while I was pregnant with my baby boy. Call it evil or whatever you want but what you saw was the look of an angry ass bitch!"

"Yeah, I hear you," Trinity says. "You kicked the *bullshit* outta ol' girl, though!"

They share one final laugh before saying goodnight and Maribel stumbles up to Dolo's door.

As soon as he opens the door Dolo is greeted by the scent of alcohol seeping through her pores.

"Drunk again," he says, disappointed. "I thought you agreed to slow it down."

"I am, baby, but when I go out I like to have a drink..."

"Or four, or five or six. I don't see why you can't go out without drinking."

"Oh God, can I at least get a damn hug before you start lecturing me?"

Dolo opens his chiseled arms and allows Maribel to fall into them. He wraps them around her and squeezes tightly. The feeling of her petite yet curvy body against his makes tolerating the scent of the liquor worthwhile.

"I'm sorry, Love. I just hate to see you tearing yourself up like this."

"I'm not, babe. And trust me, this headache I got is punishment enough for the drinks."

When he releases her he steps back to take in her sexy ensemble and notices the blood on her shoes.

"What happened?" he asks, pointing at the red splatters she clearly missed. "Why do you have blood on you?"

"Remember that girl Brittany I told you about? The one that—"

"Yes, I remember."

"Well, she was there and when I saw her I just lost it. I went off on her."

"Wow," he says, taking a seat on the couch. "Bad enough you're in clubs all the time, drinking and staying out all night. But now you're fighting too? I feel like I don't even know you anymore, Maribel."

"What the hell do you mean, Dolo? Did you forget what she tried to do to me and my unborn child? The bitch had it coming!"

"Yes, she tried to harm you, but she did not succeed. And now you've stooped to a level just as low. I don't know if it's this Trinity girl you've been hanging with or Shawn's father, but one of them is having a bad influence on you. You're changing for the worse."

Listening to Dolo lecturing her is bringing up bad memories of her boring old biology teacher from 10th grade, and it's only making her headache more severe.

"You know what," she says, massaging her temples with her eyes closed tightly. "I was really looking forward to seeing you tonight, Dolo, but now I just feel like I wanna go and get some sleep. Would you take me home, please?"

"Of course," he says in a gentler tone. "I'm sorry, Love. I've had a long day so I may be a little on edge. You're right; it's probably best if we sleep it off and talk tomorrow when we're both in better spirits."

Chapter 22

Maribel struggles to stay awake during the ride home to Tony's. She would have immediately dozed off if she didn't have to direct Dolo there. She has him let her out up the road and walks the rest of the way to the large gates enclosing the estate.

Maribel removes her shoes before entering the house and closes the door lightly. She realizes her attempt to slip in quietly and unnoticed is pointless when she finds Tony sitting on the couch, wide awake, with no company or TV to occupy him. Just his cigar, Hennessy Black on the rocks and his thoughts.

"Hey, baby," Maribel smiles, making her way over to him. "I decided not to spend the night at Trinity's. Wanted to come home and see you instead." His failure to return the greeting, along with the stern expression he maintains, instantly concerns her. Tony butts out his cigar in the marble ashtray and downs the remainder of the Hennessy in his glass before standing to face her.

"Have fun tonight?" he asks as he removes the signature "TD" initial cufflinks he wears daily and proceeds to unbutton his shirt.

"Yeah, it was cool. Same ol', same ol'." Tony takes his shirt off and folds it neatly before setting it down on the couch.

115

"So nothing eh, I don't know, *unusual* happened?"

"Well…" she begins, realizing he obviously knows something about the Brittany incident. "I did run in to that bitch Brit—"

"Tell me something, Fancy," he says, cutting her off mid-sentence. He steps closer to her and looks her directly in her eyes. "Do I look like a fool?"

"Huh? Wha—"

"Do I look like a fucking fool?"

"No, Tony. Of course not."

"Then WHY THE FUCK ARE YOU TRYING TO PLAY ME LIKE ONE?!"

In a flash Tony's fist forcefully meets her face and she finds herself stumbling backward, trying to regain her footing. The pain takes a few seconds to set in and it is not until she feels the aching sensation of her cheekbone that it begins to register in her mind that she has just been punched.

"I know about the dude you been fuckin'!" a furiously enraged Tony yells.

Maribel bolts toward the staircase when she sees him coming toward her with his fist cocked back. She manages to make it up a few steps before he grabs her ankle and pulls her down. Her chin lands hard on one of the steps, bumping subsequent ones as she's dragged downward. Tony yanks her to her feet and slams his fist into her face once more, this time hitting her so hard her vision blurs.

"You thought you could fuck me over, Fancy? Tony De Luca has eyes every-fucking-where! You can't take a piss or a shit without me knowing about it!"

"Tony, I'm so sorry! Please stop!"

"You're one dumb ass broad, I'll tell ya that! I take you out the 'hood, give you the world, and you're out here runnin' the streets, givin' up MY pussy...for free!" Tony hits her with another blow, this time drawing blood from her lip. "I tried, Fancy. I really tried. I wanted us to be a family and I gave it my best shot. But I guess that's what I get for trying to turn a ho into a housewife; trying to treat a ghetto 'hood rat like a queen. Aye, what am I saying? I should've known you were a whore. You fucked me the same night I met you!"

Her attempts to block his punches are futile. He pounds away at her, boxing her defenseless 125-pound frame as if he were hitting a grown man. She squeezes her eyes shut and curls into a ball hoping each painful blow that lands on her body will be the last. She imagines she must look exactly how Brittany looked just a few short hours ago. She feels helpless and defenseless against her ruthless attacker, and guesses this is the same way Brittany must have felt while she repeatedly kicked her, preventing her from getting up off of the floor.

"Tony, stop! Please! I'm sorry!"

"Goin' to see the dude in MY fuckin' car. Talkin' to him on the phone I pay for. Didn't you realize I could access the call and text logs, dumb ass? Matter of fact gimmie my goddamn phone back." He rummages through her purse, trying to locate her iPhone. "Actually I think I'll just take the whole bag since I bought that too. What's this? Louie? I'll give it to my new broad. Find a chick that deserves shit like this. Wait a minute. Didn't I buy that dress you're wearing? What the fuck is that? Chanel or some shit? Whores like you don't deserve to wear nice designer dresses. Take it off!" She does as she's told and begins peeling off the dress. "Everything you got on I fucking paid for! Take them panties off, too. I want them back and that bra you got pushing your tits up. Gimmie all my shit back, bitch. Tell Dolo to lace you, clothe you and feed you. At least make him earn the pussy."

She continues stripping, feeling as worthless and humiliated as Tony intends. Her desperate wailing is joined by Shawn's cries from upstairs in his room. But Tony is as unmoved by their infant son's screams as he is by Maribel's tears and repeated apologies.

"I'm sorry, Tony!"

"Yeah, I can see that. Just look at you! Go ahead, take a look at yourself," he says, pointing to the large oval mirror hanging on the wall. "I SAID LOOK!" She peers at her naked reflection. Her hair is a tangled mess and her battered face is swollen and bruised, stained with blood and running mascara. Tony grabs the back of her neck and pushes her face up against the mirror. Her face throbs painfully against its cold, hard surface. "Take a good look. You ain't lookin' so fancy now, huh? You ain't shit without me. You're nothin' but trash."

"I'll give you everything back," she sobs after he releases her neck. "Just let me get Shawn and we'll leave right now. Please."

"You ain't goin' nowhere. You ain't leaving and you ain't taking my son away from me. Now get the fuck outta my sight."

She sulks up the stairs, doubled over in pain, gripping her aching right side. She looks to the top of the seemingly never ending staircase, desperately making her way towards Shawn's cries. She can't wait to hold him in her arms and thinks it ironic that though she'll be responding to his cries, he'll really be the one comforting and consoling her rather than vice versa.

"Oh yeah," Tony yells up the staircase at her. She cringes at the sound of his voice, preparing for another verbal assault. "I hope you know that dude is married."

Married?! The word stops her dead in her tracks, letting Tony know she is unaware of her secret lover's marital status.

"Oh daaamn, you really didn't know? Yep, you ain't nothing but a jump-off!" His obnoxious bellowing laugh roars up the staircase.

Chapter 23

The following morning Maribel awakens to Shawn cries from beside her. She had brought him in her room the previous night because she felt he'd be safer sleeping next to her. After Tony's violent behavior toward her, she knows she simply can not put anything past him. When she tries to sit up she experiences pain in practically every part of her frail body. The bedroom door flings open and she grips Shawn close to her bosom to protect him. Tony walks in with the saddest look he can muster and drops to his knees.

"Baby, I'm so sorry. I let the alcohol take control of me last night. I was just so hurt by what you did. I overreacted. I should've never put my hands you on. I love you! Please forgive me." He tries to hug her but she dodges his grasp and, clutching Shawn closely, runs into the adjoining bathroom, locking the door behind her.

"Leave me alone, Tony!" she yells over Shawn's loudening cries.

"Will you please just hear me out? I was overcome with anger. And the liquor just turned me into a maniac! You know that's not like me. I wasn't myself last night. I'll never hurt you again, Fancy – I swear! I love you with all my heart!"

"That's what you said the last time you hit me!" Looking in the mirror at the nasty bluish ring around her left eye and the crusted blood on her busted lip has her reliving the horrible encounter all over again. She wonders if she'll ever be able to look into a mirror again without recalling her face being smashed into its reflection and Tony's cruel words echoing in her head. *"You're nothin' but trash."* As the words replay over and over in her mind, she finds herself thinking perhaps Tony was right. *Maybe I am just trash. I did him dirty and he had every right to be mad. I deserved what he did to me.*

"I was just so upset when I found out about you messing with that dude behind my back. I tried so hard to make you happy and to be a good father for Shawn. All I wanted was for us to be a happy family. You broke my heart, Fancy."

Maribel can hear him sniffling and his voice cracking as he speaks. She slowly unlocks the door and eases out of the bathroom. Seeing a grown man cry is a first for her – something she knew happened but, prior to this moment, had never actually witnessed with her own eyes. The image of a man as powerful and masculine as Tony bawling like a baby immediately turns her into a walking pile of guilt.

Everything he's saying is true. He tried so hard and in return, I shitted on him. She silently rubs his back to console him and when he looks into her eyes with tears streaming from his, the floodgates open and she joins Shawn and his father in tears for what has turned out to be one big family cry-fest.

"Will you give me another chance?" Tony asks.

"Yes," she sobs, "but only if you give me another one."

Once everyone has finished crying and all the tears are dried up Tony tells Maribel he has some good news for her.

"Aaron's dead."

"What? Are you joking?"

"No, it was all over the news earlier this morning. Somebody got at 'em in the prison. Shanked him up good."

"I wouldn't say that's good news."

"Why the hell not? I thought you hated him."

"I do. I mean I did. I hated what he did and the way he treated me, but I wouldn't have wished death on him."

"So you wouldn't have killed him yourself if you'd have had the chance?"

"No."

"Well, that's karma for ya. He took two innocent lives and had to pay for them with his."

"I guess so."

Tony says he'll watch Shawn for the rest of the day to allow Maribel to bum the day away. She is in so much pain she is unable to do much anyway. Her day consists of a long soak in the Jacuzzi, popping extra strength Tylenol, and lots of sleep.

When she wakes up a little after 6:00 PM, the house is completely silent. She sees that Tony has returned all of her things to her and left them on the dresser. The first thing she grabs is her cell phone from her bag to call Tony and see where he has taken Shawn.

"Hey, where you guys at?" she asks when he answers.

"Over at my ma's house for dinner." The loud mixture of Italian accented voices and dinnerware clinking tells her he is telling the truth.

"Damn Tony, I told you I wanted to go next time you went. You're always raving about how great her cooking is. When am I gonna get to try it?"

"How about I bring you a plate back tonight?"

"Well, all right. But I want to meet her, Tony. And your brother and sisters and everyone else. All this time and I still haven't met your family. That's crazy!"

"I know, I know. But I knew you're weren't feeling too good, and plus—" he lowers his voice conspiratorially, "your face...you gotta let it heal first."

"Oh...yeah, I guess you're right. But, don't forget my plate, okay?"

"Of course not."

"Buon appetito!"

"Ha ha! That's my girl. Grazie! See you soon."

Satisfied that Tony is away from the house and occupied, the first thing she wants to do is talk to Dolo and get to the bottom of this marriage business. But just as she is about to tap the "call" button, she remembers that Tony has access to the call logs and will be able to see if she phones Dolo. Text is out of the question as well, since he can also view all the numbers she has texted. *But what about e-mail?* She wonders. *There's no way he can access my e-mail through the phone company.*

She taps the web browser on her phone, logs into her Yahoo e-mail account and composes a message to Dolo: *Tony found out about us and spazzed on me last night. Can't text or call. And I can't believe you're MARRIED! :*(How could you do that to me???*

His reply comes two minutes later: *It's not what it seems. I need to see you so I can explain. When/where can you meet me?*

Maribel considers the risk she will be taking if she opts to meet Dolo. What if Tony finds out? He might actually kill her. But she is too curious about the whole marriage thing and determined to get answers to her questions. The fact that Dolo did not deny the accusations means it must be true. She is not sure how he could possibly explain it, but she knows she has to get to the bottom of it.

Next Maribel dials Trinity.

"Hey, Trin. You hear about Aaron?"

"Yeah girl, I heard. How do you feel about it?"

"I honestly don't feel anything at all. Tony was acting like I should be celebrating or something. I'm not happy about it, but at the same time I'm not sad about it. I feel absolutely…nothing."

"Well, you ain't gotta be happy. I'm happy enough for the both of us! That asshole got what was coming to him. I hope he burns in Hell."

"Oh, I'm sure he is. Anyway, I need a favor, girl…"

Trinity agrees to take Maribel to meet Dolo at the King of Prussia Mall; she e-mails him back to let him know the time and place.

Maribel's cover-up job with her make-up is subpar, so despite the setting sun, she dons a pair of Cavalli shades to hide her black eye. A strategically placed swoop of hair helps conceal the bruising on her cheek, but anyone looking closely enough can see that she is a battered woman.

Having employed similar tactics to hide bruises of her own, Trinity is not the least bit fooled by any of it. She immediately notices her friend's busted lip and demands she remove the sunglasses.

"So how long he been hitting you?" Trinity asks, in a voice as nonchalant as if she were asking the time.

"First time," Maribel lies. "And the last."

"Yeah, sure…keep telling yourself that."

"He only snapped because he found out about me messing with Dolo. He was heated and

125

he'd been drinking so he wasn't in the right state of mind."

"Let me guess – this morning he apologized, begged for forgiveness, and promised it would never happen again? Told you he loved you and even shed a tear, I bet."

Maribel sits silently, looking down at her phone.

"He probably made you feel low as shit, like it was all your fault. Am I right?"

"It was my fault! If I hadn't been fucking with Dolo—"

Trinity shakes her head and chuckles. "Baby girl, you better get away from him *now*. You know how many times I went through the same thing with Vin? Every time was 'the last time'. You know! I'm sure you remember me showing up on your mom's doorstep looking just as bad as you look now. Every time I went back to him and every time he beat me worse than the last time. It didn't stop til' I left him for good. And I didn't leave til' he put me in the hospital. But girl, you got a seed to think about, too. I know you don't want Shawn growing up motherless. Tony might even hurt *him* one day."

"Enough, Trin! Just shut up and drive, please." Maribel has her mind made up that her situation is nothing like Trinity's. She provoked the pain and punishment Tony inflicted upon her. He only did it in response to her actions and he promised that he will never, ever do it again. All she has to do is make sure he doesn't find out that she is meeting Dolo. She knows she's got to be thorough about it and not raise any red flags that will make Tony believe she's been anywhere other than where she claims. A couple of snapshots of her trying on clothes texted to him should alleviate any concern of her whereabouts. While Maribel meets Dolo in the food court at the mall, Trinity shops for a few random things for Maribel to take home.

Dolo's face shows a mixture of hurt and anger when he sees his lover's normally beautiful face is now swollen and bruised.

"He hurt you? Why didn't you tell me he hit you? I will kill him!"

"No, you won't do shit, Dolo! This is the last time you'll ever see me. Why didn't you tell me you're married?! How could you look me in the eye and lie to me like that? You said you loved me!"

"I do! You're the only woman I love."

"So what are you gonna tell me? You're separated? Getting divorced? Do you have kids? You probably have a whole damn family somewhere you're not telling me about! How come I never saw any of her stuff at your place?"

"She doesn't live with me. It's not that kind of marriage."

"Then what kind of marriage is it, Dolo? Because it would have been nice to know that all that time I was dealing with a damn married man!"

"Shhh, quiet down, Maribel. I only married her for—"

"For what? Money? Is she rich or something?"

"For citizenship," he whispers.

"Huh? I'm confused. You told me you were brought to the states by aide workers."

"I was. But when the war ended we were to be sent back to Africa. Becoming a U.S. citizen was the only way for me to stay here."

"Oh," says Maribel, feeling somewhat salty but also relieved. "So who's this woman you're married to and why are you still married after all this time?"

"She's someone I met while I was working at the car wash. The fee we agreed upon was $15,000. I've been paying her gradually, a little at a time, but while I was in school I couldn't afford to give her much, so that slowed me down. I'm almost paid up now though."

"And then you'll get a divorce?"

"Yes, Maribel. Although I'm not really sure what difference it makes. Me and her have no feelings for each other whatsoever. It's strictly a business arrangement. You're the one shacked up with your abusive baby's father even though you're supposed to be in love with me."

"I do love you, Dolo. You know I do!"

"Then leave! Pack your things and you and Shawn can move in with me."

"It's not that simple! Tony is Shawn's father. He will be devastated if I take his son away."

"Look at what he did to you! Was he as considerate of your feelings when he was pounding away at your face? The man is abusive!"

"I know that's what it looks like, but he's not. He just snapped because he found out about me seeing you. Plus, that's a major change, Dolo. Something like that requires time."

"Change is good. Sometimes you need change to be able to move on." Dolo lets out a long breath of defeat, realizing he is not getting through to her. "Look Maribel, for the past five months I've been giving you my all and only getting half in return. I'm tired of playing second position. We don't spend time like we used to. I can't see you when I want to; only when you're able to sneak away. And now you're telling me I can't even talk to you on the phone or text you? I'm sorry, but I can't do this anymore. If you can't leave him, we can't continue to see each other." Dolo gets up to leave but she stops him, grabbing his hand in protest.

"No! You can't do this! I need you, Dolo."

His heart melts at her dismal expression and he can hear the sheer desperation in her voice. She looks like a sad puppy dog – the kind with a dark ring around one eye – and he knows she is right about her needing him. But as bad as he wants to be there for her, he knows he must stand his ground. He can not continue to torture himself.

"I'm sorry. I can't keep seeing you and being there for you only for you to go home to him.

Do you know how much it hurts to be alone in my bed at night missing you while you're laid up with him? And how do you expect me to sleep now knowing that I can't protect you and Shawn from that dangerous and violent man? I just can't do it anymore."

Desperate to keep him from walking out of her life forever, Maribel finally gives in.

"Okay. I will leave him. But...just not right now."

"When?"

"Soon. I have to find the right time. I want to let him down gently, so there's no bad blood between us."

"Well I hope it is sooner than later. I can't wait forever. Hit me up if you need anything. Stay in contact through e-mail."

"I will."

Chapter 24

As the days pass, things in Maribel's life return to normal. Her bruises heal and neither her nor Tony mention Dolo again. She does, however, maintain communication with Dolo through e-mail. They continue to meet up and spend time with each other whenever they are able, which has been fairly often as of late since Tony has been especially busy. He is out of the house more than usual and when he is home he is conducting meetings – things he attributes to a new multi-million dollar contract to construct a shopping mall in New Jersey. Maribel still finds his business practices to be rather strange. To her knowledge he has no office. He conducts all of his business meetings in a very casual manner: either at Dolce Vita or in his living room (of all places) and on random days (including weekends) at any hour he chooses. With their fancy suits, his employees don't even look like typical construction workers to her. But while it certainly concerns her, she is mostly glad for the opportunity to visit Dolo without having to worry about Tony watching the clock and wondering where she is.

One evening, however, when her and Shawn return from Dolo's, there are more cars than ever parked outside in front of the house. Even during his largest meetings there are never as many vehicles on the property. The loud music and buzz of chatter and laughter let her know that a party is going on inside. But Tony hadn't mentioned anything to her about hosting such a large gathering, and she wants to know why. She furiously yanks the front door open and is greeted by a Flo-rida song blasting through the stereo system, accompanied by the distinct aromas of marijuana and cigar smoke clouding the living room air. Despite the noise, Shawn remains fast asleep; he doesn't even stir. There are people everywhere, dancing, talking and drinking concoctions poured from the many bottles of liquor and champagne Tony has provided from his extensive collection. She recognizes some of them as his workers, but she is less than pleased at the quality of the women present. They are all gorgeous, fit and fashionably dressed – Barbie types – nipped, tucked and painted to photo-ready perfection; the kind of females most women would love to be or be seen with, but certainly do not want anywhere near their men.

She finally makes her way through the crowd of drunken strangers to the couch, and her jaw drops when she sees Tony reclined on the leather sofa, a glass of scotch in one hand, a Cuban cigar in the other, and a beautiful, perfectly stacked brunette on his lap.

"Um, HELLO Tony! What the fuck is goin' on?"

"What's it look like?" he asks, both him and his curvy companion looking at her as if she is crazy. "It's a party! Now take my son out of here with all this smoke and noise." He makes no attempt to explain nor remove the woman on his lap.

"Who is this bitch and why the fuck is she all up on you?!"

"Excuse me?" the brunette says with attitude, leaping up and opening her arms confrontationally. "Who are you calling a bitch?!"

"Chill, chill, Rita," Tony says, pulling her back down onto his lap and rubbing her back to calm her down. "That's just my son's mom. Don't mind her. She's about to leave."

"No the hell I am NOT leaving! Tony, if you don't get that skank ho off of you right now—"

"You'll do what, Fancy? Take your ass to your room, and take my son outta here before he wakes up. It's late. Put him to bed."

"NO! Tell all these people to go, Tony!" she screams in frustration, feeling helpless and on the verge of tears. He ignores her, turning his attention back to the woman on his lap.

Maribel storms up the stairs, lies Shawn down in his crib, closes his bedroom door and trots back down the steps and over to the stereo system, yanking the cords out of the wall. When the music stops the chattering also dies, and the party guests turn their attention toward her, each wondering who's the killjoy that stopped the music. Finally, all eyes are on her and she has the floor to speak.

"That's it!" she says, clapping her hands and swinging the front door wide open. "Party's over. Time for all of y'all to get the fuck out of here!

Thanks for coming and don't let the door hit you on the way out."

"Hold the fuck up!" an outraged Tony yells, pushing the woman off his lap and storming over to Maribel. His first reaction is to punish her for her blatant disrespect in front of his audience. But he calms down and recomposes himself when he remembers his father's words: "A true boss never lets anyone see him lose his cool." He decides to give her one final chance.

"Fancy," he says to her, speaking slowly and in the sternest of tones to make sure she comprehends him, "You need to chill out right now. My guests aren't leaving and if you keep this shit up, you're gonna be embarrassed in front of all of them. Now I'm gonna tell you one more time – take your ass to your room."

"NO!" she yells in his face, crossing her arms and pouting like an immature little girl standing her ground against her strict parents.

As Tony prepares to unleash his wrath upon her, the spectators watch closely as if witnessing a real life soap opera unfolding right before their eyes. They are waiting for him to explode on her any second now, but before he can respond, one of the suited Italian men in the room steps between them. Maribel recalls seeing him briefly once or twice in the living room meetings, but she's never actually met him. Looking at him now, she notices he looks a lot like Tony, just a little younger.

"Tony, who the fuck is this broad? You got her shackin' up with you or something?" Tony turns away in embarrassment and says nothing.

"Yes, for your information I do live here. I'm his girlfriend and the mother of his child!" Tony's guests begin to leave as they realize the music is not coming back on and the party is over for good. The juicy soap opera has turned into an episode of Maury they've already seen, and at this point, they would rather change the channel than watch the buzz-killing baby mama drama transpiring between Tony De Luca and his live-in girlfriend.

"Is this true, Antonio?" the man asks. "Is this Li'l Tony's mother?" Tony looks down at his Armani shoes as he shuffles his feet restlessly.

"Li'l Tony?!" Maribel yells. "My son's name—"

"Is it?!" he demands, before she can finish her sentence.

"Yes! Okay? It's true," Tony says, finally looking the man in the eye. "She's his mom."

"Well that explains a lot. Now I see why you never brought her around. I bet Pop is rolling over in his grave. He glares at Tony with disdain, shaking his head, then scowls in disgust at Maribel. "What did Pop aways tell us, huh? '*You can fuck whoever you want but when you marry or make a baby, it damn sure better be with an Italian girl.*' And this is how you honor him? You taint the De

Luca name by giving it to your half-breed, bastard son? You're a disgrace to the whole family."

"It was an accident, Francesco! I didn't fuckin' do it on purpose."

"Well. At least now we know we can take you out of the running to take over as capo."

"I'm the first born son, damn it!"

"That doesn't make you the right person for the job. You've proven yourself unworthy."

Francesco is the last person to leave and as he walks out the door shaking his head he says, "Ma is gonna be so disappointed in you…her oldest son. Way to represent the family."

Maribel stands silently in shock, trying to process all that just happened. The treatment she had received from Tony was deplorable. Not only had he disrespected her in front of dozens of people, he actually had the audacity to allow a female to sit comfortably perched on his lap while she stood right there. Then there were Francesco's hurtful words, compounded by Tony's shameful response. He didn't bother to stand up for her or even defend his own son. He made it quite obvious that he is completely ashamed of them both. Seeing no point in arguing, Maribel storms upstairs to her room and begins to pack up her clothes. Tony is fast on her heels.

"What the hell you think you're doing?"

"What does it look like I'm doing, Tony? I'm getting the fuck out of here! It's over! You think I'm gonna stay with you after the way you just treated me? You embarrassed me in front of all those people. Just acted like I was nothing to you. Let that slut sit right on your lap and didn't even want her to move when I walked in. But never mind me. Let's not forget the way you allowed your brother to talk about our son! You stood right there and let him call Shawn a half-breed bastard! I've never been so disrespected in my whole life."

"*Me* disrespecting *you*? The only reason I started seeing Rita again is because you've still been talking to that Dolo dude! Still up to your same tricks."

The statement throws Maribel for a loop. She wonders how on earth he could possibly know that. *Probably just guessing. Taking shots in the dark to try to justify his own actions.* She decides that in the absence of proof, it's best to just deny it for now.

"I have not seen Dolo and anyway, why would you care? There's no future for you with a non-Italian like me. I can't believe you didn't tell me your family was so prejudiced! Keeping me hidden away for all this time. What did you do? Tell them Shawn's…oh wait, no…"Li'l Tony's" mom was Italian? How long did you think you could lie until the truth came out?"

"How long did you think you could keep sneaking off to see dude behind my back?! I told you I have eyes EVERYWHERE! You even took my son with you on your whoring escapades!" Outrage is written all over Tony's beet red face as

137

he inches toward Maribel with his nostrils flared and fists balled. She backs up against the wall, attempting to brace herself for the unleashing of his fury upon her once again.

"Why the fuck do you continue to take me for a joke?" he asks, slowly creeping toward her. "I would have thought you'd have learned your lesson the last time. What do you want, huh, Fancy? You wanna push me to the limit? Is that it? You wanna see how mad you can possibly make me? Mad enough to put a bullet through your thick skull? Mad enough to cut you up and send the pieces of your body floating down the Schuylkill River? Nah, I won't do you like that. With you it's personal. I'd rather wrap my hands around that pretty little neck of yours and squeeze the life out of you. Watch your eyes so I can see the look in them when you take your last breath. Yeah, I'm pretty sure you won't be satisfied 'til you're dead." By now he is smiling satanically and whispering in Maribel's ear in a menacing tone as she quivers in the corner. "You *want* me to kill you! Like I did Bella...and Aaron...and Brittany."

"Oh my God, Tony! YOU killed Bella and Aaron?! And Brittany's dead too?"

"Yeah, Brittany's recently deceased. R.I.P.," he says nonchalantly, "but don't worry...nobody will ever find her body. And I didn't personally kill them, but yeah, they were problems of yours that I had taken care of. I told you, nobody gets away with trying to bring harm to me and mine. I did it for you, Fancy, because I loved you. I would have done anything for you. I even went out of my way to make sure we could be together. That little fire at your mom's house...I did that just to get you and Shawn in here with me. Isn't that romantic?"

"Tony how could you?! You're crazy! I ca—"

Her words are cut off as Tony firmly grips her neck with both hands. He squeezes tightly, instantly blocking the flow of air through her trachea. She desperately claws at his fingers, struggling to get free, but he only clenches harder. Eyes bulging out of their sockets, she is still aware of what is happening, but her attempts to stop the strangling in progress are completely useless. She can feel her flailing body weakening more and more with each passing moment. No longer able to control her bodily functions, her bladder involuntarily begins releasing a constant stream of hot urine. And when she defecates on herself, she is sure she is dying. She is helpless and the lights start to dim as her oxygen-deprived brain slowly slips into unconsciousness. She closes her eyes and allows her body to go limp, finally giving in to the death that is coming.

Just then the house begins to rumble as if an earthquake is shaking it. Piece by piece the cracking floor starts crumbling beneath her body until it opens up completely and swallows her whole. She falls into the blackness and can feel the flames of Hell getting hotter as she nears them. Suddenly, someone grabs her arm, stopping her fall. She looks up and is momentarily blinded by the bright white light. She squints at the dark silhouette, trying to make out who has reached down to catch her. It is Shawna grasping her wrist with both hands, desperately trying to save her from the flames growing by the second, and attempting to pull her up to Heaven.

"Fight, Maribel, fight!" her best friend yells down to her. "You can join me here. There's still time!" But she doesn't fight. She lets her body hang heavy until Shawn is no longer able maintain her grasp. Her wrist slips through Shawn's fingers and Maribel watches Shawn spread her wings and fly toward the light as her limp body descends into Hell to be consumed by the fiery pit of flames.

Maribel regains consciousness gasping for air on the carpeted floor soaked with her urine. She sits up in the dark room realizing that she is, in fact, still alive in her room at Tony's house. It's not Hell but it's close enough and she doesn't plan to spend another night here. Grimacing at the foul stench of her own feces and ignoring her soiled clothing, she grabs the partially packed bag on her bed and runs into Shawn's room to retrieve him. He is still fast asleep in his crib when she leans in to scoop him up in her arms.

"Going somewhere?" Tony's voice resounds from a dark corner of the room. He leans forward in the rocking chair he'd been reclined in, and his menacing face is illuminated by the stripes of moonlight streaming through the cracked blinds. His demonic grin sends a cold chill running down her spine. Cradling her sleeping son, she runs toward the staircase, but Tony catches her by the arm and spins her around.

"You're not taking my son from me. I'll kill you before I let you leave here with him." She believes him. She knew he was violent from the beatings he inflicted on her, but knowing now that he is responsible for the deaths of Bella, Aaron and Brittany, as well as the fire at her mother's house, she realizes he is even more ruthless and dangerous than she ever could have imagined.

"Go to your room, Fancy." She would not dare disobey him now and risk angering him while holding her son. She does as she's told and saunters back down the hall with Tony right behind her. Once inside the room, Tony fishes her phone from her bag.

"You won't be needing this anymore. From now on you don't leave this house. I don't even want to see you outside this room unless you're going to the kitchen. The only reason you're alive is to take care of my son. You try to run away and I'll kill you. And don't even think about trying to call for help. You go near the phone, you're dead. Understand me?"

Having no choice in the matter, Maribel nods in agreement.

Tony heads downstairs and Maribel sticks her head out the cracked door into the hallway to eavesdrop on his conversation with Bo.

"Bo, keep an eye on her. Make sure she doesn't leave the house and I don't want her anywhere near the phone."

"You got it, boss."

Chapter 25

Maribel's first few days of being a prisoner confined to the house are tough. Her initial thought is to try to get her hands on one of Tony's guns. She waits until she hears him exit the house and pull his car through the gates before tiptoeing carefully down the hall to his room. She turns the doorknob and pushes on the door, but it won't budge. She jiggles the handle, hoping it is only stuck, but her worst fear is confirmed; Tony has had a lock installed on his bedroom door, making it impossible for her to gain entry.

"Hey, what's goin' on up there?" Bo's voice bellows up the staircase. As she dashes back to her room she can hear his massive footsteps pounding up the stairs. She quietly slips under the sheets and closes her eyes right before Bo flings open her bedroom door.

"Jesus, Bo, can't you knock? You scared the crap outta me!"

"Oh…uh…sorry. I thought…"

"Can't even get a decent nap in around here!"

With her plan of getting ahold of a gun thwarted, Maribel decides that her only chance of ever escaping captivity rests in somehow getting downstairs to the phone in the living room. It is the only landline in the house and if she manages to get to it somehow, she can call the police and tell them she's being held hostage. The plan is to sneak a quick call in while Bo is outside on a cigarette break, but she also needs to be sure Tony is out of the house first.

Over the next few days she listens out for the sound of the front door opening and keeps a log of the beginning and end times of Bo's smoke breaks. The idea is to gauge the frequency and length of time he is outside, so she can better calculate how long she'll have to get downstairs, make the call and get back upstairs before he finishes his cigarette.

Listening out for a door to open is just about the most boring thing a person can do. And being as though that is one of the only things Maribel has to occupy her time, her days and nights are painfully dull. She imagines this must be how prisoners in solitary confinement feel. The only human interaction she has is with her infant son and she longs for some sort of companionship or adult conversation. Maribel has never been a huge fan of TV, but finds herself much more appreciative of the tube now that she has nothing but time on her hands.

One evening she is watching the news and her heart stops when she sees a face so familiar, she is sure her eyes must be playing tricks on her.

"Tony?!" A photo of him appears on the screen adjacent to pictures of two other men as the reporter begins the story.

Key witnesses scheduled to testify against mobster Antonio De Luca, Jr. were found dead in the East Falls section of Philadelphia last night. The bodies of two men pulled from the Schuylkill River shortly after 9 PM, each with multiple gunshot wounds, have been identified as Jake Buccelo and Michael Mercado. Both men planned to testify against De Luca in court this coming Wednesday as he stands trial facing a slew of charges, including conspiracy, racketeering and money laundering, as well as drug and arms trafficking. De Luca, son of the late notorious mob boss Antonio De Luca, Sr., denies any involvement in the murders.

The news segment cuts to recorded footage of Tony giving a brief quote as he makes his way through a sea of journalists, cameras flashing all the while. "It's such a tragedy," he says into a reporter's microphone, giving his best attempt at appearing and sounding genuine. "My sincerest condolences go out to the families."

Maribel sits stunned, trying to make sense of it all when she is suddenly startled by movement behind her. She turns and sees Tony standing in the doorway.

"I look good on TV, don't ya think?"

"I knew something was up with you. Had a feeling that construction crap was bullshit."

"Well yeah, I might have embellished a little about the construction stuff, but I was telling the truth about working in the family business."

"Some respectable business that it. The business of drugs, crime, extorting and killing people."

"Don't speak on things you know nothing about. My great-grandfather dedicated his whole life to building the De Luca empire. Don't knock it. It's the business that keeps a roof over your head and food in your mouth. The business that'll ensure Shawn never has to want for anything."

"What about a real father? One that's a good man and makes an honest living?"

"As much of his time as my pop invested into the business, he still always made time to be the best damn father to me and my siblings. He taught me and my brother how to run the biz just like I'm gonna teach Shawn."

"Really? Even though he's not full-blooded Italian? How'd the family take that news?"

"He's still a De Luca," Tony says after a brief hesitation.

"Hmmm last time I checked he was an Alvarez."

"He's my son and he has De Luca blood running through his veins! His name will be changed."

"Never. Lucky for him you'll be in jail soon."

"Ha! You saw the news. None of those charges will stick with those finger-pointing rats out of the picture. Besides, I got the best lawyers money can buy and I'm sure you're aware that I'm very well connected. I ain't goin' nowhere." Tony strolls confidently out of the room, pulling the door closed behind him.

Maribel knew Tony was hiding something but it had never occurred to her that he could be a part of Philadelphia's Italian mafia. In retrospect so many of her concerns about Tony are explained by this one discovery: the guns, the money, the need for so much security; even the "eyes everywhere" and the strange meetings with suited "construction workers."

This is too much, she thinks, as she begins to feel faint. She sits down on the bed, holding her head with both hands as if it will stop all the thoughts from swirling within it. She hopes her opportunity to get to the phone comes soon, but now she knows calling the police will not be wise. She remembers the photo on the mantle of Tony looking chummy with the police commissioner, so despite the charges being brought against him, it's still probable that he has some of the police force in pocket. With all that has happened, she believes *anything* is possible and concludes that calling the cops could potentially jeopardize her and Shawn's safety. *Back to the drawing board.*

Chapter 26

It doesn't take long for Maribel to formulate Plan B, and a few short days later, when Tony takes Shawn out, she seizes the opportunity to begin implementing it.

Once Tony and Shawn are gone, she patiently awaits Bo's first cigarette break and cracks her door to listen out for the sound of the front door opening. From keeping logs of Bo's smoke breaks, she knows she has a maximum of four minutes to get downstairs, dial, complete her call and get back up the staircase.

When at last she hears the familiar sound of the door's squeaky hinge, she jogs quickly but quietly to the top of the staircase. After peeking down to make sure Bo has finished exiting the house, she sneaks past the cracked front door and over to the end table where the phone rests. Her adrenaline is pumping and she knows if she is caught the repercussions will be lethal. She takes a deep breath to relieve her shakiness and, in a hurry, she picks up the receiver and dials the number embedded in her memory. Thankful that Trinity has answered quickly, she nervously begins rattling off.

"Trin, it's me – Maribel."

"Where the hell you been? I haven't been able to reach you on your cell."

"I don't have a lot of time so listen closely. And this is gonna sound really crazy but it's the truth. Tony took my phone and is holding me captive in his house. He's crazy, dangerous and on top of that I just found out he's part of the mob. I need you to help me get out of here."

"Holy shit, girl. Do you want me to call the cops?"

"No! Whatever you do, don't do that. He probably has 'em in pocket already. I need you to get in here and do something for me."

"There?"

"Yes, here – in Tony's house. I need something from his room but he keeps the door locked. You can get in though, and help me get what I need."

"How the fuck am I supposed to do that?!"

"Well, you know…seduce him with your feminine charms."

"Are you serious?"

"Yeah. He's a man. He likes jawns. Foolproof plan. There's an Italian restaurant on Locust called Dolce Vita. He's always there. Usually goes around 7 or 8 for dinner. Hang around there in the evenings and catch his eye. Come on to him and get him to take you home with him."

"But I don't even know what he looks like. How am I supposed to know him when I see him?"

"He's good looking and fit with black hair. Cocky mothafucka'. Walks like his shit don't stink. He'll be wearing a sharp suit and stepping out of something fly—a black Rolls, white Benz or green

Maybach, most likely. And he'll definitely be wearing diamond TD cufflinks."

"Okay. Then what?"

"Put his ass to sleep and when he's finally out cold I need you to get the .357 from the top drawer in his nightstand…it's the shiny gold gun with the black handle. Bring it down the hall to my room. It's the room closest to the staircase."

"A gun though, Maribel? What you gonna do with that? Have you ever even used one before?"

"I shot one once at the range with Aaron."

"Shit, girl…I don't know if I can do this. What if he catches me?"

"He won't! You can do this, Trin – you have to. You owe me. Do this for me and Shawn. Please. You're our only hope."

"Okay, okay…I'll do it. So all I have to do is get you the gun, right?"

"There's more."

"More?! Like what?"

"I need you to take Shawn out of here."

"That impossible! How am I supposed to take the man's son out of his house without anyone seeing?"

"Bring a large bag. That tan Michael Kors tote you got will be big enough. He'll be in my room with me so when you pass me the burner, we can set him in there."

"And then what? Where am I gonna take him?"

"To Dolo. I gotta go now, but please Trin, you gotta do this for me. Go down Dolce Vita tomorrow night and every night until you see him."

"A'ight girl, I got you."

Maribel places the phone onto the receiver and hustles back up the stairs, just before Bo steps into the house.

Chapter 27

The following two nights are disappointments. Tony comes home with a different girl each night, but neither of them are Trinity. The days seem to get longer and longer as she keeps her sights focused out the window and her ears open, watching, listening and waiting patiently. The walls seem to close in on her, making the room and house smaller with each passing day.

Around 11 on the third night, Maribel's ears perk up when she hears two cars driving through the gates. The cars have already passed her line of sight before she makes it to the window, so as Tony and his guest enter the house, she presses one ear against her bedroom door, crossing her fingers in hopes that the companion Tony has brought home is Trinity. She looks up and mouths a silent "thank you" to God when alas she finally hears her friend giggling up the hall with her son's father. Now all she has to do is wait.

She soon hears the sounds of sexual activity and is content knowing that all is going according to plan. When the moaning and headboard banging finally stop, she knows it won't be long until Tony is fast asleep. She swaddles her sleeping son in a blanket and cracks her door, waiting for Trinity to make her move.

After a half hour, Trinity appears at her door and hurries into her room. She hands over the gun she has retrieved, and Maribel immediately checks to make sure is loaded before tucking it safely under her pillow for the time being.

"Look what else I found," Trinity whispers, holding out her closed hand. Maribel's eyes light up when Trinity drops her beloved heart locket necklace into her hand.

"You found it!" Maribel gasps. "Oh my God...thank you, Trin. I thought I'd never see it again." Inspecting the necklace, she is not surprised to learn that Tony never fulfilled his promise to have its chain repaired. She supposes he never intended to fix it or return it to her. Maribel puts the locket in her pocket before taking the diamond teardrop necklace from the dresser and handing it to Trinity.

"Here, take this."

"Gladly," Trinty says, admiring the sparkling pendant.

"I don't want any reminders of him after I'm gone." Finally, Maribel lifts Shawn, who is still sleeping, from the bed. She kisses him softly and sets him gently inside Trinity's tote bag.

"Be careful with him, Trin."

"Of course."

"Here," she says, passing Trinity a folded piece of paper. "Make sure you give this to Dolo. It's very important."

"Okay."

"Thank you, girl. Thank you so much."

"Be safe," Trinity replies. They hug briefly and Trinity is on her way. Maribel watches anxiously through her window and lets out a huge breath of relief when Trinity's car pulls safely through the front gates. *No matter what happens to me at least Shawn will be safe.*

Maribel wastes no time setting the rest of her plan into motion. She calculates that she should try to leave in about an hour to allow for ample time in case something should go awry. She spends part of the hour packing, and the remainder of it restlessly pacing back and forth across the floor, mentally psyching herself up for the task ahead of her.

When 1:30 AM rolls around Maribel is set and ready to go, with her duffle bag over her shoulder and Tony's gold .357 tucked into the waistband of her black jeans. She waits for another of Bo's smoke breaks to descend the staircase and make her way toward the back door, located in the kitchen. Bruno will be guarding the back door, as usual, and as she slowly nears the kitchen, she realizes she is in way over her head.

What the hell am I doing?! I'm about to pull a gun on a mafia soldier who's probably been shooting people longer than I've been alive. What if he doesn't drop his weapon when I tell him to? Then I'll have to try to shoot him before he shoots me. Even if I hit him first, gunshots will alarm the whole house, and my chances of getting away will be ruined.

All the pep talking and hyping up in the world couldn't prepare her for this. Heart beating quadruple time and sweating like a pitcher of lemonade at a summer barbeque, she steps to the end of the hall. She hears the flat-screen television on in the kitchen and imagines Bruno sitting in his chair, gun on his waist, waiting to do what he does best...kill. With her back flat against the wall, she closes her eyes and says a silent prayer. She takes one final deep breath, dries her sweaty palms on her pants, and removes the gun from her waistband. This is it, she thinks. It's now or never.

Like a TV detective Maribel whips around the corner, instantly taking aim square at Bruno's head. He doesn't move. He is sound asleep, slumped over with his mouth wide open and a drop of drool dangling from the corner of his bottom lip, slowly making its way to the large wet spot on his shirt.

Well I'll be damned. Quiet as a porch mouse, she slowly tiptoes across the kitchen floor, watching Bruno's eyes to make sure they don't open. His chair is sitting diagonally in front of the door, allowing for only a narrow passageway. Lifting her duffle bag over her head, she sucks in her stomach as tight as she can to avoid brushing up against Bruno or his chair. She exhales once she successfully clears the chair. Now the task at hand is to open the door, which she can see is not going to be an easy feat with the chair being so close to it. She unlocks the lock, turns the handle and gently tugs on the knob until the door opens. Little by little, she continues pulling the door open wider until it has opened as far as it will go and is up against the back of the chair. Inhaling deeply again, and holding her breath to make her body as slender as possible, she begins sliding through the narrow opening. She feels her breasts being painfully pushed and squeezed, until finally, the pressure of the door on the chair causes it to shift quickly, it's legs squeaking against the kitchen floor as it jerks. Bruno jumps slightly, grumbling as he readjusts his posture and Maribel stands frozen and petrified, stuck in the doorway with her heart threatening to pound right through her chest. Once Bruno settles back down, she slips the remainder of her body through, quietly closes the door, pulls her black hoodie over her head and takes off running across the grass. With the hardest part of her escape behind her, Maribel's climb over the iron gate is practically a cake walk, and after accomplishing it with minimal scratches, she's as free as a bird. When her feet are finally firmly planted on the soil outside of Tony's estate, she looks up into the starry night sky, thanking God for her freedom and her remarkable good luck.

Chapter 28

Walking along the side of the road with only the slight glow of the moon and stars to guide her, Maribel wishes she had considered a flashlight. She squints, straining her eyes, and looks far down the road, searching for the lights that will let her know she is nearing her destination. Seeing nothing but the black night sky ahead of her, she picks up the pace, increasing from a brisk speed walk to a jog.

When she turns around and sees headlights approaching from behind her, she starts to panic. *What if Tony woke up and noticed me and Shawn are missing?* She realizes her plan was not very well thought out. It was flawed, leaving loose ends that could easily be discovered before she gets a chance to arrive safely to her destination. The vehicle is getting closer and closer. She frantically tosses her bag into a ditch on the side of the road and jumps in after it, laying down flat so that she is no longer visible from the road. After the car passes, she sticks her head out of the ditch to see if she recognizes it, but it is too dark to tell. All she can see is its red taillights and she doesn't climb out of the ditch until they've completely disappeared.

After trekking on for another half mile, Maribel is relieved when she sees the fluorescent lights of the Exxon gas station on the horizon. With her destination finally in sight, she puts even more pep in her step and runs the rest of the way there.

But instead of going straight up to the gas station, she waits in the driveway across the street from it, attempting to stay hidden in case Tony or one of his men happen to come looking for her.

She looks at her watch. *2:37 AM. He's late!* The anxiety returns once more. *What if he's not coming? What if he wasn't home? Oh my God. How will I get to Shawn if he doesn't come?!* She impatiently glances at her watch again and does so about twenty times within the next three minutes.

At 2:40 – ten minutes later than she had calculated – Dolo's gray Charger pulls into the gas station. Maribel wastes no time running over and hopping in the passenger side, first looking into the backseat to make sure Shawn is safely strapped into the extra car seat she kept at Dolo's.

"I'm SO glad to see you!" she tells Dolo, giving him a tight hug and long kiss before they pull off.

"I'm just glad you're safe, Love."

"You were 100% right about Tony. I should have listened when you tried to warn me. That man is a violent, dangerous psycho! Can you believe he's part of the mob?!"

"Yes, Trinity told me everything."

"I have to go someplace where he can never find me and Shawn."

"I'll make sure that he doesn't. I'm going to keep you both safe."

"But how, Dolo? He has people everywhere. And the first place he'll probably look is your house. I didn't mean to put you in danger, but I didn't know who else to turn to for help."

"You were very brave to do what you did and you did the right thing by sending Shawn to me. You know I love you both and would never let anything happen to you."

"But where can we go now? Do you have anything in mind?"

"Well, you know I'm due to go home in a couple weeks. Come with me. We can stay and start a new life there."

"Come to Liberia? For good? What about your job? I don't even have a passport."

"Calm down," he chuckles. "We'll find a way to make it work. We will have to get rush passports for you and Shawn. In the meantime, we can just lay low somewhere. Maryland, upstate New York—"

"Connecticut. After all this I wouldn't mind seeing my mom."

"You don't think he'll look there, knowing you have family living there?"

"Connecticut is a big state. I never mentioned what city they were in. And besides, my aunt has a different last name – her husband's – and since he's not a legal citizen here, they're not listed anywhere. They fly so far below the radar it would be impossible to find them."

"Okay then. We can go see your mom, and just to be safe we'll stay in a hotel in one of the neighboring towns until we get you and Shawn's passports situated."

"Sounds good to me," says Maribel, placing her hand on Dolo's. "Thank you for everything."

"Let me ask you something, Maribel," says Dolo as he turns the car onto Route 309. "What does your ideal future look like? Paint a picture for me."

"Well, just like you said, my ideal future includes you, me and Shawn living somewhere safe where we can start a new life; someplace where I won't have to constantly look over my shoulder and wonder if Tony is coming after us. I want to finish getting my nursing degree and work at a hospital. I would love to work in a maternity ward like you, taking care of mothers and their newborn babies. I plan to keep being a good mom, raising Shawn right, and making sure he has a nice life. That's really it, Dolo. I just want a normal life. I want to move on and leave all the drama behind. And I want you by my side while I do it."

"That sounds...perfect," Dolo says, turning to look into her eyes. "Let's do it."

Maribel squeezes his hand and a huge smile stretches across her face as she gazes back into the eyes of the man she loves. Dolo reciprocates the gesture with his own sparkling smile and her heart skips a beat. She glances at her sleeping angel in the back seat and is content knowing that he will be safe and that they are finally on their way to true happiness.

Chapter 29

Gunshots are fired, snapping them out of their daze and shattering Dolo's back window. Maribel and Dolo had been so entranced with each other they failed to notice the nearing headlights of the car speeding up behind them.

"Get down!" Dolo orders, flooring the gas pedal.

"Fuck! It's Tony!" Maribel slithers into the backseat with Shawn, who is screaming and bleeding from several cuts made from the shards of glass. Her heart breaks at the sight of her baby boy in pain. Her blood boils with hatred for Tony. She removes the gun from her waistband and aims it out the opening where the rear window used to be, firing a shot at Tony's car. She manages to shoot out the windshield and James swerves and accelerates, pulling up beside them and attempting to ram them off the road.

"Pass me the gun!" Dolo orders. "Get up here and take the wheel."

"I don't know how to drive!"

"Just steer the wheel! Keep us on the road. This will only take a minute."

When Maribel is back in the passenger seat, steering the car, Dolo wastes no time. He lets off three expert shots, one for each of the men.

Tony's car spirals out of control before finally crashing about 50 feet up the highway from them. Dolo pulls up behind the car, leaving his headlights on to illuminate the crash.

"Wait here," he says to Maribel, as he exits his vehicle, gun in hand, to see if anyone has survived. His inspection reveals that James has been hit in the head. He most likely died instantly, causing the car to crash. Bo barely clings to life in the passenger seat, dazed from the accident and the loss of blood from his severe chest wound. He desperately gasps for air, choking on blood as he continues to rapidly bleed out. Dolo looks into the backseat for Tony. He is nowhere to be found, though pools of his blood remain. The right rear door is open, so Dolo follows the trail of blood through the grass until he finds Tony slithering off into the field, attempting to flea the scene.

Tony turns when he sees Dolo's large shadow hovering over his weakening body.

"You must be Dolo," Tony says through bloody teeth. "Trust me, you don't wanna do this, bro. You kill me now, you'll be dead tomorrow. Let me go and I'll make sure you're taken care of. Money, protection, whatever you want – I can make it happen for you."

Emotionless, Dolo raises the gun and prepares to squeeze the trigger.

"Wait," says Maribel, walking up behind him, holding Shawn in her arms. "Let me do it."

"Are you sure you want to? Once you take a man's life, you're changed forever."

"A wise man once told me that change is good. Sometimes you need change to be able to move on."

Dolo silently hands her the gun and takes Shawn into his arms.

"Say goodbye to Daddy," she says, as Dolo starts back to the car with the baby.

Once Dolo and Shawn are safely inside the vehicle, she averts her attention back to Tony, who has been busy begging for his life all the while. She turns back just in time to catch him saying, "You can't kill me, Fancy. You love me. Please..."

She points the gun at his face and stares into his desperate eyes as they fill with tears. Crippled and bloody, Tony looks so helpless and fragile. His body trembles and tears fall from his eyes as he continues to plead for her mercy.

"Please! Don't do it, Fancy! Don't kill me."

A sudden feeling of pity overcomes her and her hand begins to quiver as she feels her nerve threatening to slip away.

"You know what, Tony? You're not even worth it." She lowers the gun and begins to walk away from him. To Maribel's surprise, Tony immediately erupts into laughter. She turns back to find him with his head tossed back like a wolf howling at the moon. He looks at her with a sinister smile to taunt her one last time.

"I knew you didn't have it in you, you stupid bitch. You couldn't possibly shoot me. You're no killer. But go on, now. Run off into the night. I will find you and I will kill you. And I won't stop there. I'm gonna kill Dolo too…and your mother. I'll make sure you all die the slowest, most painful deaths imaginable. But don't worry about Shawn…I mean Li'l Tony. He'll grow up to be great like his father, and I'll be sure he knows exactly why and how I killed his mother…Fancy." Again, Tony's roaring laugh resounds, echoing all around her.

Now Maribel peers at him without a trace of sympathy in her eyes. Eyebrows close, she looks down at him with pure disgust and hatred. The pity she felt for Tony just moments ago is now nonexistent. Now, instead, his taunting and laughter has once again reminded her of the true monster that he is. His weak and injured body reminds her of her own reflection after the repeated abuse she sustained at his cruel and merciless hands. She knows he means what he says and has every intention of carrying out the torturous murders he speaks of.

"You will never see me or my son again!" she yells, raising the gun once more and pointing it at his face. She steadies her shaky hand by bracing it with her other hand, before turning her head and closing her eyes tightly. She squeezes the trigger and after the bang of the revolver, all she hears is the thud of Tony's lifeless body falling over onto the ground. She turns to look at what she has done. The once handsome features of his face are no longer recognizable. All that remains is a bloody mess of tissue, muscle, bone and brain matter. She twists up her face at the gruesome sight. "And it's not Fancy," she spits at the corpse. "It's MARIBEL!"

Chapter 30

The next morning Maribel awakens in Dolo's bed, snuggled in his warm and protective arms. The two of them had decided that with Tony out of the picture, there was no longer an immediate threat preventing them from resting up and returning to gather a few of Dolo's things before heading to Connecticut. They weren't sure if permanently relocating to Liberia was still necessary, but they figured it would still be wise to lay low out of town for a while, just in case Tony's brother or anyone else in his camp had any suspicions about her being involved in his murder.

Dolo doesn't stir while Maribel wriggles out of his arms and hops out of bed. She peeks over at Shawn, who is also still asleep in a makeshift bassinet she fashioned from a laundry basket. She laughs quietly to herself. He sure didn't have any problem getting a good night's sleep in there, after such a fiasco. Luckily, aside from the few nicks from the window shattering, he seemed to be unaffected by it all.

She goes to the kitchen to start breakfast, wanting Dolo to wake up to the delicious smell of bacon and eggs. She leaves the living room television on as she cooks, keeping her ears open for a story about Tony. As planned, the delightful aroma eventually wakes Dolo, and he walks into the kitchen holding Shawn. She gives each of her handsome guys a good morning kiss and sets the table so they can eat. When they hear the news anchor mention Tony's name, they migrate into the living room to see what the police have made of his death.

Antonio De Luca, Jr., son of the late notorious mob boss, Antonio De Luca, Sr., was found slain early this morning in Lower Gwynedd Township, alongside Route 309 North. Although police have no witnesses, authorities have speculated that De Luca's death was a result of internal conflict and feuding within the De Luca family. There is reason to believe the murder was an inside job as power within the mob changes hands. Since the death of Antonio, Sr., there's been heavy debate within the family regarding who will replace him as the head of the mafia, a position that now, in the wake of the death of Antonio, Jr., seems likely to fall on the youngest De Luca son, Francesco.

Maribel exhales deeply in relief, happy to know she will have a chance at a new beginning. It has been a long journey. She has been through a whirlwind of strife, chaos, confusion and pain, but at last, she feels confident knowing exactly what she wants and where she is headed. All is finally right. Maribel and Dolo exchange silent smiles and she hugs him and Shawn close, optimistically looking forward to the rest of her life.

THE END

Coming soon from Hope Street Publishing

THE CITY OF BROTHERLY BLOOD

A novel by Vanna B. and Cal Akbar

Chapter 1

He's been here before. He opens the door and is met by the stale aroma of cigarette smoke and spilled beer. Cold and unfamiliar stares from yellowed and bloodshot eyes at the bar slowly turn to greet him as the stranger makes his way over to the pool tables in the back. The lounge, Smitty's, is a dimly lit tattered relic from the Seventies that was once a popular hangout for local pimps, hustlers and high rollers. Those days are long gone now, and the crowds of people who once filled the spot seem to have disappeared with disco music, bell-bottoms and the Black Power Movement. The lounge's condition mirrors that of the remaining patrons scattered about the place; what was once bold, brilliant and lively is now lackluster, dilapidated and dying. Alone at one of the two pool tables adjacent to the restrooms, stands the man the stranger has come to see.

A slender ebony-skinned man is his mid-sixties leans over the table, a pool stick gripped in his arthritic hand, preparing to take a shot. The rusty brown plaid shirt he wears is rolled up at the sleeves and on one arm he bears a dull gold watch. The watch, which looks to be around the same age as its wearer, shows its scratched face and catches the eye of the young man who approaches the table. He's seen that watch before. The young stranger slips both his hands into the deep pockets of his oversized olive green army jacket.

The old man slowly draws back the stick and with a loud, sharp crack sends balls flying about. The scuffed orbs shoot violently across the table and come to a slow halt, none falling in a pocket. With a smile he looks up at the young man.

"It ain't what it used to be."

The stranger smiles back. "Your pool game?" asks the younger man, as he pulls a lighter from his pocket and a Newport from behind his ear.

"Naw," answers the old man, squinting at the stranger, the smile fading from his face. "Everything."

"We've met before," says the old man. "You look like somebody."

"Nope, don't think so. Not from around here."

"Maybe I know your father."

"Maybe...but he dead."

"Oh. Sorry to hear that."

"No need. My pop died when was young...never knew him, really." The stranger lights the cigarette. "Wanna play a quick one?"

"Sure," replies the old man. "Rack 'em."

The stranger loosens his grip on the cool metal of the heavy handgun he palms in his pocket, and picks up a pool stick before setting up the balls for their game.

"Not from Philly, huh," says the old man, more as a statement than a question. "What brings you to this dump?"

"Just passing through," replies the stranger. "Wanted to see what this town had to offer."

"Well this here ain't it. This place hasn't been worth shit since the Seventies. You should head on down to South Street or Center City. That's where all the action is. This place here is a certified shithole now."

"You gotta be kidding me," the young man muses, raising his eyebrows and looking around sarcastically. "This looks like a pretty classy establishment to me."

The old man chuckles. "It may not be much to look at now, but back then it was the place to be."

Chapter 2

It's August of 1975. It's a packed house at Smitty's Lounge. The sound of music, chatter and laughter fills the air. Red leather booths with black piping are along one wall and on the other is a long mirrored bar spanning from the front of the lounge all the way to the back where two pool tables sit.

At one booth is Bobby "The Duke." A neighborhood pimp known for his tall stature and short temper, Bobby sits at the table with a woman on each side. He pours a glass of champagne from a bottle and hands it to the woman seated to his right. The Duke calls her Prissy, which is short for Priscilla. Bobby decided some time ago that the name Priscilla was "not a suitable name for no ho." And "Besides," he concluded, she was "one fine, prissy mothafucka'."

Prissy is a young girl with bronze skin and silky black hair down to her plump behind, both of which she inherited from her Dominican mother. A short white dress clings to her firm thighs and white patent leather knee boots are on her feet. Prissy is undeniably gorgeous with the looks and sex appeal of a Hollywood starlet, and she might have become one if she did not come from a broken home with a heroine addict step-father who used her mother for a punching bag and Prissy for a sex toy.

Prissy had fallen madly in love with The Duke. She wants nothing more than to please him, even if it means hopping in cars with strange men and performing sex acts for money. She stares silently into her untouched glass of golden fluid, watching the tiny bubbles rise and solemnly recalling the past.

Three years ago it wasn't like this, she thinks. She was a shy sixteen-year-old when she met Bobby. It was a cold December afternoon when he pulled up alongside her in his pearly white Cadillac as she was briskly walking home from school. It was the same route she had taken home every day, but she had never before seen the handsome curly-haired older boy around her neighborhood in North Philadelphia. He smiled at her as the dark tinted windows dipped low, and to Priscilla, it was like the cool gloom of night being chased away by the glow of the morning sun. She was instantly filled with glee.

Priscilla was stunned that a pretty boy like Bobby with such a fancy car would stop and talk to her. At sixteen she wasn't much of a looker, she thought. Her skin was oily and her messy hair was stuffed under a wool hat. The dingy tan coat she wore was coming apart at the seams and so were her tennis shoes. Prissy hurried off, trying not to look back at the car.

Needless to say her first encounter with Bobby would not be her last. Every afternoon for a week the shiny white Cadillac would appear with its charismatic driver offering to give her a ride. The Duke reminded her of an actual duke that she read about in history class. He was a feudal lord galloping on horseback courting a poor peasant girl as she toiled the field. He said his name was Bobby and insisted that he would not stop coming around until she went out with him.

Priscilla knew better than to accept rides from older, smooth-talking boys with expensive cars. She heard stories about girls who got in cars with strange men and were never seen again. Yet Bobby seemed like a nice guy to Priscilla and despite her better judgment, one grey afternoon when icy, freezing rain fell from the sky, she could no longer decline his offer.

In the beginning it was different. Bobby was the quintessential gentleman. A sharp dresser, meticulously groomed with a melodic way of talking that was reminiscent of a preacher in a pulpit. When The Duke spoke it was like he was giving a Sunday sermon and every time he paused to take breath, one got the urge to fill in the gaps with an "Amen" or "Hallelujah."

"Priscilla," he repeated when she had first told him her name. "Pris-cilla" he echoed again slowly. "I dig it," he said. "It has a nice ring to it."

Months later, after a brief courtship and countless sexual encounters; after Bobby convinced her to drop out of school and run away from home; after he turned her out and had her selling her body on the streets, the name Priscilla had long lost its "nice ring."

Nowadays she never hears her birth name.

She goes by the name The Duke gave her.

"Prissy!" barks The Duke, his voice snapping her out of the trance. "Bitch, why you sittin' there lookin' all sad and shit? It's your birthday." She looks up from her glass and forces a smile.

"Yeah girl," adds the female sitting on the other side of The Duke. "This is your day. You ain't got no damn business moping around." The female is Charmaine, another of The Duke's girls. Charmaine is a pudgy chocolate girl who wears shoulder length curls. She was once a high school cheerleader with aspirations of becoming a dance choreographer. When she met The Duke a little over a year ago, she put those dreams on hold for the promise of fortune, jewelry and furs, and has been turning tricks for The Duke ever since.

The form-fitting black blouse Charmaine wears is cut low and the tops of her huge, round heavy breasts stick out, threatening to spill over at any moment. "Girl, finish that drink," she insists, reaching across the table to pass Prissy her glass. As she lifts Prissy's drink, one of her massive globes breaks free from its bondage and flops out of her blouse. Charmaine jerks back her arm to clutch her exposed breast, spilling the glass of champagne on Prissy and knocking the entire bottle over onto the table.

"Shit, bitch!" exclaims The Duke, resisting the urge to backslap her. "Watch what the fuck you doin'!" The Duke's bracelet collection dangles from his wrist as he points his jeweled index finger. "Wipe that shit up! Got ya titty all on display and ain't even no john around. I swear you gots to be the dumbest bitch a pimp done ever had."

Embarrassed, Charmaine squeezes her breast back into her blouse, apologizing in a sheepish, childlike tone.

Prissy, grabs a napkin and stands up wiping her dress. "It's alright, Char. It'll dry." She is only half upset with her friend and co-worker. In the year she has known her she has come to expect random acts of clumsiness from Charmaine. Besides, it gives her an excuse to leave the table and be alone with her thoughts.

Prissy makes her way back to the restroom and both male and female patrons can't help but steal glimpses at the angel in heels as she slinks by.

At the bathroom sink, Prissy stares into the mirror and tears are forming in the eyes of the face that stares back. Today is her nineteenth birthday and it marks yet another year of her whoring for The Duke. *It isn't supposed to be like this*, she thinks. *It was supposed to be a temporary situation.* According to Bobby, she was to help them get on their feet by turning a few tricks and that was it. Bobby promised they would have a bright future together but three long years have gone by and that future is nowhere in sight. He promised them a legitimate income, a house and children. The promises he made were all but broken – *except for one*, thinks Prissy as she rubs her belly. Because inside of her, grows a life and that life is the product of Bobby, The Duke.

Chapter 3

Smitty, sitting only a couple tables away watches as Charmaine's breast flops from her blouse. Holding back his laughter he prods his partner Lex with an elbow trying to get his attention but by the time Lex looks over in the direction of the pimp's booth, Charmaine has already holstered her breast. What Lex sees is a drunk and furious Bobby, The Duke looking as if he is about to lash out at one of his girls.

In an instant, Lex springs to his feet, ready to strike. Smitty recognizes the fiery look in his right hand man's eyes and sticks an arm out in front of Lex's chest.

"Whoa brother," says Smitty. "Be cool."

"That mothafucka' knows the rules," snaps Lex.

The "rules" that Lex is referring to are the rules posted in bold red letters on a sign by the entrance to Smitty's Lounge: Rule number one: No guns. Rule number two: No fighting. Rule number three: absolutely, positively no bullshit, whatsoever.

To Lex, The Duke appeared to have been about to violate both rules number two and number three, and he was more than happy to enforce them if the pimp felt inclined to make an infraction.

Lex watches as The Duke shakes his gold ornamented fist at Charmaine, threatens her with a whisper and calms himself down. Disappointed that he will not get to rough up the pimp, and satisfied that The Duke is not about to go into a violent rage, Lex eases back down into his seat.

Smitty's attention is not on The Duke at all. He is confident that he will not start any commotion in the lounge, not after the talk that he and Lex had with him a while back. What Smitty is focused on is the half-Dominican bombshell in white that sits at the booth with The Duke.

Smitty sits at his table with Lex, Lex's girlfriend Marie, and Marie's friend Sonja. Marie brought Sonja along with the hopes of hooking her up with Smitty, but his attention appears to be elsewhere. Smitty, usually the social butterfly, is quiet and introspective this evening. He watches as Prissy rises and sashays to the restroom, and as she walks by he inhales deeply though his nostrils hoping to catch even the slightest whiff of her perfume through the fog of tobacco smoke. Excusing himself from the table, Smitty follows behind her.

"What's up with Smitty?" asks Marie, noticing the folded arms and agitated look on Sonja's face.

"He cool. Just tired," Lex replies, lying to Marie with a straight face.

"Hey baby girl," says Smitty, creeping in on Prissy as she is putting on lipstick in the restroom.

"What are you doing in here, Smitty? You don't belong in the women's restroom."

"I own the place, mama. I can go wherever I

please," replies a grinning Smitty as he creeps up behind Prissy to encircle her in his arms.

"Smitty! I already told you," says Prissy, pushing him away. "I'm The Duke's girl."

"I ain't come in here to change your mind, baby. Just wanted to give you something." Smitty reaches into his back pocket and pulls out a small velvety black box. "Happy birthday, baby girl."

"I can't take this," says Prissy, quickly pushing the box away.

"Whats wrong, Priss?" A puzzled and stunned Smitty looks down at box he cradles with both hands. "You okay?"

"I aint been drinkin', Smitty. You think you can just come into my life and get my head all mixed up? I have a man."

"He's your pimp, Prissy. He doesn't care about you."

"Oh and you do? He takes care of me."

"I'll take care of you. You don't need him."

"You think you know me, Smitty? You think because you fucked for free we got some kind of connection?"

Smitty opens his mouth to speak but the words get caught in his throat.

"Well we don't!" snaps Prissy.

Smitty can sense something is wrong with Prissy. He was more than just some trick that picked her up on the street. It had started out as a night of sex but it developed into what he thought was an attachment they both shared for one another. They spent countless nights together "off the clock" with her in his arms. They talked about the past and discussed future plans. Smitty consoled her when the tears poured from her eyes. She'd always refrain from talking about Bobby, but she opened up to him and shared countless stories from her troubled childhood. One story in particular always sticks with Smitty. As Prissy told it he could barely contain the anger that it stirred within him. Smitty remembers the account vividly.

When she was nine years old, there was a corner store at the end of her block. The store, owned and operated by an old Puerto Rican guy named Pedro, was a typical bodega selling groceries, candy and other goods.

"I had this yellow summer dress with daisies printed all over it," she recalled. "That dress was one of my favorites but it had a loose button near the top that just wouldn't stay fastened and so it kept slipping down over my shoulder. I wore that dress one day when my mom sent me to Pedro's to grab some bread. He pulled me behind this curtain leading to the back of the store where he had a room with an old mattress in it. It looked like he pulled that mattress right out of a dumpster, it was so dirty. Wasn't made up at all; no sheets, no pillows. I remember him climbing on top of me. His breath smelled like licorice and cigarettes and he was grinning from ear to ear. He had this one shiny gold tooth with a spade engraved in it, but the rest of them were yellow and nasty. I shut my eyes but that awful smile and that gold tooth stuck in my head. To this day I still have nightmares of him smiling in my face with that tooth and his hot breath on me." The tears came. "I was a little girl, Smitty. I didn't know no better. I wish I never would've worn that stupid dress!"

"It wasn't you fault, baby. It wasn't the dress," Smitty said, rubbing her back. "Did you tell anyone?"

"No. I was too scared. I didn't think anyone would believe me. The whole neighborhood loved Pedro and they still do."

"You mean he is still there?" asked Smitty.

"Yeah, he's still there. No telling how many little girls he took to that back room."

Probably still taking girls back there, thought Smitty.

Prissy had a horrific childhood. Given the circumstances, its no wonder she got mixed up with a man like The Duke. When Smitty looked at Prissy he didn't see Prissy the prostitute, he saw a scared girl who sought shelter from the storm but instead got sucked into the whirlwind of the streets.

Still, Smitty didn't know how to react to Prissy's sudden change of heart. Rejection was something he was not accustomed to. Perhaps The Duke found out about the two of them spending time together and threatened her with violence. Whatever the case, something was definitely wrong.

"Look, Smitty, you are a really nice guy. We had some good times together and I thank you for being a shoulder to lean on, but Bobby needs me. I am not gonna run out on him. I can't accept your gift and I don't think we should see each other anymore."

"Bobby doesn't give a shit about you, Priss!" Smitty exclaims. "He's a mothafuckin' parasite that lives on the blood of young girls. He's a piece of shit!"

"Oh and you so fucking high and mighty, huh? You ain't no saint, Smitty. I've heard stories about you and ya little friend Lex. You done a lotta shit far worse than Bobby, I'm sure."

"You can't believe everything you—" The door cracks open.

"Prissy, Bobby wants to know what's taking you so long," Charmaine's high-pitched voice comes from behind the parted door. She peeks her head in and sees that Prissy is not alone. "Oh...um, sorry. I didn't know."

"Its fine, Char," says Prissy dryly. "I was just leaving."

Smitty clenches his teeth, squeezing the jewelry box in his fist and shaking his head in disbelief as Prissy struts out. With a deep sigh he walks over to a stall, opens the black box, and tilts it over the toilet. The gold tooth with a spade etched into it falls out of the box into the bowl and with a flush, it disappears.

Thank you for reading *Fancy 2*!

If you enjoyed this book, please leave a review for it on Amazon and tell a friend about the *Fancy* series.

You can connect with me on social networks and subscribe to my newsletter, as well as the Hope Street Publishing newsletter, via the web addresses below.

<u>Vanna B</u>:
www.facebook.com/vannabonline
www.facebook.com/fancybyvannab
www.goodreads.com/author/show/5828871.Vanna_B_
www.twitter.com/msvannab
www.instagram.com/vannab215
www.youtube.com/vannab215

<u>Hope Street Publishing</u>:
www.HopeStreetPublishing.com
www.facebook.com/hopestreetpublishing

Hope Street Publishing
P.O. Box 2705
Philadelphia, PA 19120

About the Author

Vanna B. is an author and publisher of fiction novels. The Hope Street Publishing CEO is a native of Philadelphia, PA and received her BA in journalism from Temple University. Writing has been a life-long passion of hers and she always planned on authoring books.

Vanna's professional writing career began with newspapers and magazines, where she served as a restaurant reviewer, proofreader, advice columnist and staff writer covering a range of topics including current events, local politics and culture. After making the decision to leave the workforce to stay home to raise her son, she began penning her first novel, *Fancy*.

Fancy went on to be a huge success, landing on the Amazon Kindle best-seller's list for multiple categories, earning Vanna the 2012 Philly Hip Hop award for "Best Author," being featured in *The Source Magazine*, and receiving overwhelmingly positively reviews.

"I'm incredibly grateful that my work is being so well-received," Vanna says. "I love writing and sharing my gift with others, and I work very hard at providing top-notch material with the goal of bringing readers a unique and memorable experience."

CPSIA information can be obtained at www.ICGtesting.com
Printed in the USA
LVOW01s2119130114

369235LV00032B/1477/P